Dedicated to my beloved wife,
Gloria Scharr,
who is the inspiration for Grandma in
this book.

Grandpa's Legacy

Andrew J. Scharr

PublishAmerica
Baltimore

First printing

ISBN: 1-4137-1255-X
PUBLISHED BY PUBLISHAMERICA, LLLP
www.publishamerica.com
Baltimore

Printed in the United States of America

Table of Contents

Introduction

The following is a collection of stories that published together form the chapters of a book. The stories are about a grandfather and his extended family, and are narrated by a grandson. The stories are fiction based on family, friends, and religious life in north Louisiana. The epilogue is narrated by a great-grandson.

I planned the first stories with the intent that hunting would be the thread that loosely held the stories together as a book. Something happened between then and now. As I read back through each chapter, I realized that instead of the thread of hunting holding the stories together, they are held together by a strong rope, which is the family members' individual and collective belief in Jesus Christ as our Savior.

Andrew J. Scharr, Author

Chapter One

In the Beginning

Our family oral history has it that our first paternal ancestor came to Louisiana in the early 1800s. It is told that he walked here with nothing but a flintlock rifle and the clothes on his back. Very little is known about this man except that he married a Louisiana girl and that they had one son. It is thought that he repaired guns for a living, didn't own land, and didn't prosper in those hard times. It is not known whether or not he attended church.

Succeeding generations of our family fell on more hard times. The War of Succession took a father and a son. The yellow fever epidemic took a father and a mother and five children. Our family did not prosper.

Along about the end of the century, a wild young man, headed for Hell, met a beautiful preacher's daughter, and was smitten by her. The price for her hand in marriage was that he attend church with her every time she went, which was every time the church door was open.

The young man paid the price and married the beautiful girl. He was exposed to God's Word in the little church, and he repented his sins and was baptized in Jesus' name, and our family has prospered ever since.

The wild young man and beautiful girl were my great-grandfather and my great-grandmother.

Chapter Two
First Grade

Grandpa's mom and dad pioneered a little subsistence farm on the edge of the Big Swamp. They raised a few vegetables and such, but mostly they lived off of hunting, fishing, and trapping in the swamp.

They weren't educated and I don't think they ever had a book in their house. But they came to realize the importance of education, and when Grandpa was old enough, they sent him to the little one-room schoolhouse five miles up the road.

Great Grandma told Grandpa that kids at school wore shoes and that he should carry his homemade shoes with him when he walked to school, and put them on just before he got there, and then take them off to walk home, so he wouldn't wear them out, because he wasn't getting another pair for a long time.

Grandpa grabbed his shoes and the little sack lunch that his mother fixed, and his single shot 22 caliber rifle, and started up the road toward the school, hunting as he went. Just as soon as he got out of sight of his home, he hid his shoes in the bushes. Grandpa couldn't tolerate shoes when he was a kid.

Just before he got to school Grandpa stopped at a mud hole in the road and coated his feet with black mud so it would look like he had shoes on.

When Grandpa got to school he put his 22 rifle in the coatroom with the other kids guns and took a seat in the first row. There were eight rows of desks in the school, and each row was a grade, first through eighth grades. When you finished one row, you moved to the next.

During "Get Acquainted," Grandpa told how he lived on the edge of the Big Swamp, and that he hunted, trapped and fished for a living. From then on everybody called him Swamp Boy, and Grandpa was proud of his nickname because he was a swamp boy.

At noon when Grandpa sat on a stump to eat his sack lunch of squirrel and cornpone, a group of the bigger boys gathered around him. The biggest boy's name was Buck, and he was a bully.

Buck said to Grandpa, "Swamp Boy, I don't bring a lunch to school because I always eat one somebody else brings. Looks like I'll eat yours today."

Grandpa's dad, my great grandpa, had done a little bare knuckle fighting at fairs and such, for money. And he had taught Grandpa that fighting was a rough, dirty business, and that he should always try to talk his way out of a fight. But if talking failed, and that if Grandpa knew that fighting was the only right way out, then he should go ahead and get it over with as fast as possible.

So Grandpa told the bully, "I'm going to count to ten and if you're gone by the time I get to ten, I won't have to whip your butt."

Then Grandpa shot up off the stump like a coiled spring, and hit the bully square in the nose. Grandpa's fist broke the bully's nose, and blood came pouring out.

The bully staggered to the water pump and started bathing his bleeding nose in cold well water.

As Grandpa resumed eating his lunch, one of the other big boys said to Grandpa, "I thought you said you were going to count to ten?"

Grandpa said, "I did count to ten. I was already up to nine. And I'm already back up to nine again."

The big boys left, and never did bother Grandpa again.

After noon recess, the teacher took Grandpa into the coatroom for a private talk. She said, "The incident on the first day of your attendance at our educational facility has necessitated that I, as your primary educational instructor, do instruct you in the proper deployment of your conduct while on or about the school premises. Consequently to your violation of our no-tolerance-of-violence policy, I must place you on probation for the duration of your tenure in the first grade. Do you understand?"

Grandpa had been taught to be polite, so he answered, "Yes, ma'am." Even though he had never before heard most of the words that she used.

When Grandpa came out of the coatroom, the other students asked him what the teacher had said.

Grandpa said, "I reckon she said that she approved of the way I whipped the bully, and that she thought my new black shoes looked nice."

Actually, Grandpa's black feet were starting to look more like worn-out shoes as the mud dried and fell out from between his toes.

When school let out for the day, Grandpa grabbed his 22 rifle and hunted his way home. He killed one fat fox squirrel on the way. And just before he got to his house, he retrieved his homemade shoes from the place where he had hidden them, and he went on to his house.

The first thing that Grandpa's mom said was, "How was school?"

"I think I'm going to like first grade," Grandpa said.

And he was right. Years later Grandpa always said that the first grade was the best three years of his childhood.

Chapter Three
Bootleggers

Before Grandpa met Grandma, he was wild and he was reckless, but he didn't break the law. In those days, there was very little law in Grandpa's region of north Louisiana. And what little law there was, was slow and mostly stayed in town, and never went out into the big swamp.

Making moonshine whisky was a common practice and nobody seemed to mind very much until some outsiders came in and started selling an inferior and dangerous kind of moonshine in the parish.

The outsiders that were selling the bad 'shine' were what were loosely known as Red Backs. They are a Gypsy like people of mixed race, that got their nickname from the dark red color of their skin, and the fact that they rarely wear shirts. I think that they mostly like to show off their homemade tattoos and their knife fight scars.

The local residents knew that the Red Backs came and went by boat into the Big Swamp. So when livestock and personal property started disappearing at the farms near the boat road into the swamp, the locals got together and asked Grandpa to check it out. Grandpa was raised in that area.

From the way the boat road ran, Grandpa figured that the Red Backs were set up on the Bear Knoll. The Bear Knoll was a high place in the swamp that could be walked to in dry weather, but it was an island in the wet season.

After dark that night Grandpa slipped his John boat into the water of the boat road, and paddled and poled his way to the Bear Knoll. As he approached the knoll, he could see the campfires of the Red Backs. It looked like about three families were camped there.

Grandpa slid his boat up on the mud and walked to the edge of the firelight. All activity in the camp stopped as the Red Backs began to realize he was standing there.

"What do you want?" one of the men said in a thick accent with pronunciation that betrayed the fact that he had never seen the words written down.

Grandpa drew his big Bowie knife from his belt and flipped it up in the air. The knife rotated end over end three times and landed with the handle in the palm of his hand, and the razor sharp edge pointed up, and the point pointed towards the Red Backs.

Now, most all serious social activities the Red Backs took part in, included the use of a knife. And if there was anything in the world that the Red Backs recognized, it was the stance of a skilled knife fighter. And Grandpa was in that stance.

The Red Backs' knives were usually the long slender, quick opening pocketknife variety. They took one look at Grandpa's big Bowie knife shining in the firelight like a mirror, and they left their pocketknives in their pockets.

Grandpa said, "Come daylight there won't be any Red Backs in this Parish."

Then he turned and left.

Grandpa lingered just out of the firelight long enough to observe that the Red Backs were hurriedly breaking camp and loading their gear into their boats. They were well out of the parish by daylight.

Later on, Grandpa ran into the sheriff in town and the sheriff said, "I heard you ran the Red Backs out of the parish a while back. How'd you do that?"

Grandpa said, "I just talked to them in a language they understood."

Chapter Four
Genealogy

Grandpa was wild and reckless when he was growing up. His parents lived on the edge of the Big Swamp and made a living fishing, trapping, and hunting. They weren't exposed to the social graces.

Grandpa was smart and he learned well in school. And all of the girls were attracted to his rugged recklessness.

When Grandpa was in high school, there was a dance in the old gym nearly every Friday night. Some of the local boys would play the music. Grandpa never brought a girl to the dances. He usually just went for the fighting. But he always took a girl home. And it was always a different girl, until the twelfth grade when the new pastor for our church moved in with his wife and daughter.

The daughter was beautiful. But she had no eye for Grandpa, and Grandpa wasn't used to that. So Grandpa did something that he had never done before. He asked her if he could walk her home after school and carry her books for her.

The preacher's daughter said, "No."

So naturally Grandpa became obsessed with her and asked her every day if he could walk her home and carry her books. She always said, "No." Until one day she got all of her books out of her desk and even brought a few from home, and on that day she said, "Yes."

Grandpa walked her home and carried her books every school day after that until graduation, even during hunting season.

After graduation Grandpa asked the preacher's daughter to marry him, and she said that she would, if her father agreed. Grandpa was a self-assured young man, and even a little cocky, but when he went to the pastor's house he was scared stiff.

The pastor was expecting Grandpa because his daughter had told him that Grandpa was coming over, and that he was going to ask to have her hand in marriage. And she had already asked her father to say, "Yes.'

The pastor let Grandpa stammer around for a long time, and made up a real stern face, until Grandpa was sure he was going to say, "No." But the preacher said, "I'll approve of this marriage under two conditions. First, you must promise to go to church with my daughter every time she goes. It's not proper for a lady to have to go to church without her husband, and you need it and so does she. Second, you must promise to never lay a hand on my daughter in anger, and never hit one of your children. If you ever break one of these promises you'll deal with me."

Grandpa said, "I'll promise both things."

The preacher married Grandpa and Grandma at our little church and their marriage was made by God, and blessed by God. And Grandpa and Grandma were always in church every time the door was open. And Grandpa never hit Grandma or any of their children.

Grandpa accepted Jesus as his Savior and was baptized in Jesus Name, and was filled with Jesus' Holy Spirit, as Grandma already was.

And Grandpa and Grandma cherished each other until the day that they died, and ever after in eternity. Soon after the wedding the preacher and his wife went to pastor another church in a different state, and somehow over the years we lost track of them.

Lately we've been trying to put together the genealogy of our family, so we searched the courthouse records in Baton Rouge for information about Grandma's parents. The records show that Grandma's father was a preacher, and that he and Grandma's mother were killed in an accident when Grandma was two years old. And that nobody else of that surname has existed since that time, except Grandma.

We told the man at the courthouse that those records were a mystery, because Grandma's dad had pastored our church when she was eighteen years old.

The courthouse man said, "Things like that aren't unusual in Louisiana. When Huey Long ran for governor, half of the people in the cemetery cast their votes for him."

Chapter Five
The Tithe

Grandpa's oldest brother, my great uncle, was born in the last quarter of the 1800s. He declined to go to school; instead he worked on his parent's farm until he was twelve years old.

At twelve, Great Uncle was as big as most men, and as strong too. He got a job on a logging crew that was cutting cypress in the big swamp a few miles from his home. He started out as a catchall worker, and soon moved up to caring for the oxen, and then up to saw hand, with a crosscut saw.

A few years went by and Great Uncle was doing okay. He lived in the logging camp most of the time, and always sent his paycheck home to his parents.

During the wet season, when it was too wet to log, Great Uncle would hunt and fish in the big swamp. He built a hunting cabin way out there somewhere, and he got to where he would stay gone from home for long periods of time.

One summer Great Uncle had some kind of a logging accident, by which he received an injury that put him on permanent disability.

He could still hunt and fish, and every once in a while he would stop by Grandpa's and Grandma's, and leave them a deer hindquarter, or some ducks, or some fish.

But he withdrew more and more, and he got to where he would leave the deer or whatever he brought in the smokehouse, and not ever come up to see Grandpa and Grandma.

Grandpa knew where Great Uncle's cabin was, and every month when the disability check came in, Grandpa would cash it for Great Uncle, and take it to the cabin.

Grandma would always send as much as Grandpa could carry, of things like salt, or sugar, or coffee, or a blanket for cold weather.

When the water was up in the swamp, Grandpa had to go most of the way in a John boat. Great Uncle's cabin was built on a platform between three big cypress trees and the water couldn't reach it.

Grandpa would leave the bundle of food and the money, on the cabin doorstep. Great Uncle had got to where he couldn't tolerate people, and Grandpa never saw him, but the next month the bundle of food and the money would be gone when Grandpa came back.

Years went by, and then one day when Grandpa took the money and the food to the cabin, the bundle from the month before was still on the cabin doorstep, except it had been strewed all around by raccoons that ate the food.

Grandpa knew something was wrong, so he went inside the cabin.

Lying on the bunk were the remains of a frail old man with snow-white hair and a snow-white beard down to his waist. Great Uncle had been dead for over a month. It was the first time Grandpa had ever been in the cabin. Nobody except Grandpa and Great Uncle knew where it was.

Grandpa told Grandma that Great Uncle had built little shelves on all the walls, and that the shelves were full of woodcarvings carved out of cypress knees, of every kind of animal found in the swamp. There was a bear, a panther, a bobcat, a squirrel, a rabbit, a raccoon, a possum, a deer, a fox, and more, and every kind of bird, every reptile, every waterfowl, and every kind of flower found in the swamp. And they were beautifully carved.

And Grandpa said that a homemade table stood in the middle of the one room cabin, and on it was a house like a dollhouse. It was an exact model of our little country church.

Grandpa took the roof off of the little church and looked inside. He said that inside the church was an altar with a preacher preaching, and an open Bible on the lectern. And the pews were filled with worshipers. And kneeling at the altar was a man and a woman. The woman had snow-white hair piled up on her head like Grandma, and the man had Sunday bib overalls like Grandpa always wore.

And standing outside the church, peeking in the church window was a little carving of a man with long white hair and a long white beard down to his waist. And there were little wooden tears falling out of his little wooden eyes.

Grandma asked Grandpa, "Are you going to bring your brother in for burial?"

Grandpa said, "No, brother can't tolerate people." And that was that.

Many years later, after Grandpa and Grandma had passed away, we were having our annual family reunion and several of my cousins got together and said that they were going to find the cabin and give Great Uncle a decent burial, and put his woodcarvings on display in the Parish Museum.

I think that some of them believed the legend that Great Uncle had never spent a cent of his disability money, and they thought they would find it and get rich.

I knew better. I was treasurer of our church during that time, and every month somebody left an anonymous donation to our church, and it was always the exact amount, to the penny, of Great Uncle's disability check.

But the cousins went out searching anyway. They searched for days, and all they ever found was a fire-scorched place on some big cypress trees way out in the swamp.

I speculate that Grandpa burnt the cabin and its contents down on the day he found Great Uncle dead, because he knew Great Uncle couldn't tolerate people.

I speculate that God did one of two things on the day that Great Uncle got to Heaven. Either he gave Great Uncle a cabin by himself in a beautiful swamp, or he cured Great Uncle of his intolerance of people and, or, angels.

We're taught that a tithe means a tenth, and that most good Christian people try to return ten percent of the increase of God's bounty to them, back to God for his work.

Great Uncle's tithe wasn't ten percent, it was one hundred percent.

Chapter Six
The Answer

Grandpa didn't believe in celebrating Halloween, because he believed it was an anti-Christian tradition. But every year he would get the grandchildren together and tell them this true story of what happened one Halloween when Grandpa was a younger man:

Grandpa told that one October, Grandma's big lazy cat came up missing. The cat always could be found sleeping in Grandpa's front porch rocker, until now.

Next, a neighbor discovered that some of his chickens were gone. Then another neighbor discovered his bull calf was missing.

After church on Sunday, everybody was talking about the missing livestock. They speculated that a panther from the big swamp had started getting a taste for domestic animals.

The milkman, who was known to have a vivid imagination, claimed to have seen a panther cross the road ahead of his milk truck on the old swamp road.

As a group, the neighbors asked Grandpa to do something about the panther. They always came to Grandpa for help, especially if it concerned the big swamp.

Grandpa investigated the site of the chicken disappearance, and the site of the calf disappearance, and he began to form a theory of what had happened, and it didn't include a panther. Grandpa knew that the last confirmed sighting of a panther had been over fifty years before.

Off the Old Swamp Road not far from the livestock disappearances, was an abandoned farm known as the old Jones place. It was Halloween day when Grandpa parked his truck on the dirt road where the old grown up driveway turned off, and he walked the quarter of a mile in to the old Jones house. The door was ajar on the long abandoned house, so Grandpa went in. What he saw in the big living room confirmed his theory. There were chicken feathers and calf bones and cat parts everywhere. There were Devil worship signs written all over the walls in dried blood. There was a bloody altar in the center of the room.

When Grandpa turned to leave, there was a strange man blocking the only door, and there were a bunch of other strange men and women behind him, and Grandpa was trapped.

The evildoers had strange marks painted on their foreheads in blood, and they were chanting in a strange language. The men surrounded Grandpa and forced him onto the altar on his back. Then they tied his arms and legs so that he couldn't move.

The head Devil worshiper told Grandpa that they had been intending to sacrifice a child on Halloween, but that Grandpa would do even better.

The evildoers danced round and round Grandpa, all the while chanting strange words. Finally the head evildoer stood over Grandpa with a dagger raised and pointed straight at Grandpa's heart. Then the evildoer plunged the dagger at Grandpa's heart as hard as he could.

There was only one thing that Grandpa could do. He shouted, "I rebuke you in Jesus' name."

And Grandpa woke up. He was home in bed. He had been having a nightmare.

Grandpa felt over on Grandma's side of the bed and sure enough, she was there.

Grandma woke up enough to say, "Go back to sleep, old man, and don't be making any plans that can't wait until morning."

In the morning, Grandpa looked out on the front porch, and there was Grandma's fat, lazy cat sleeping in the porch rocker. And Grandpa always ends the story by saying, "This true story is to teach you that whenever you have a situation that you can't overcome by yourself, call on Jesus, and He will always answer your call, and either provide a way for you to overcome the problem, or give you the strength to endure it."

Chapter Seven
The Horse Whisperer

Grandpa didn't like to ride horses much. He said that he would rather walk on his own two legs, that horses were too much trouble. And anyway they couldn't go good in the Big Swamp.

But in Grandpa's younger days horses were a necessity on the farm, so Grandpa knew a lot about them. He knew that they would throw you, because he had been thrown several times. And he knew that they would bite you, because he had been horse bit several times. And Grandpa always said that you haven't felt a good lick until you've been kicked by a horse.

But as usual, when the neighbors had a problem they brought it to Grandpa. So they brought the horses that they couldn't break to Grandpa to break. Grandpa had a good degree of success with bad horses, and he got a reputation that he could break any horse.

So, would-be horse trainers started coming to the farm to watch Grandpa break horses.

They said that Grandpa would get his mouth right in the horse's ear and stay that way until the horse started responding to his training. Sometimes it took hours.

They said Grandpa was a horse whisperer.

Grandpa said that that was a bunch of bull. He said that he didn't whisper to the horses. That what he did was bite them on the ear as hard as he could, and not let go until he got their attention. He said that horses were a lot like people. You couldn't teach them anything until they were willing to listen. Grandpa said that he didn't really like the ear bite method of horse breaking. It left a bad taste in his mouth.

Chapter Eight
The Camping Trip

Grandpa usually went to bed soon after dark. He always said that when the chickens went to roost it was time for him to go to bed. But just after dark on Christmas Day that year, Grandpa's phone rang.

It was the neighbor down the road and he was real worried. The neighbor man and his wife had only two children, twin boys. The boys were not yet in their teens, and had gone off into the big swamp that morning and hadn't come back.

Back a few years ago, when this happened, our nation hadn't yet got caught up in the crazy anti-gun hysteria. Kids, boys and girls, were usually started off with a BB gun and when they showed maturity with the BB gun they were moved up to a real firearm, usually a single shot 22 caliber rifle, and probably handed down from an older brother or sister. That's how people were taught to control themselves.

In those days everybody had a gun and lots of people carried them all the time. And, you know, people were more polite to each other then. And you didn't hear of much robbing and raping going on.

Country kids like us would hunt our way to school in the morning during hunting season and leave our guns in the coatroom, and then hunt our way home in the afternoon. And we ate lots of wild game in those days. And there weren't any school shootings, but you can bet that if one had of broken out, somebody would have grabbed one of those coatroom guns and put a stop to it.

Anyway, the neighbor twins had received new single shot, 22 caliber rifles for Christmas that morning, and after they took another gun safety course from their father, they went off hunting along the edge of the big swamp, and didn't come back by dark.

The neighbor man called Grandpa because Grandpa knew the swamp better than anybody else, and it seems like everybody always called Grandpa when they had a big problem anyway.

Grandpa grabbed his six-volt lantern and went to the neighbor's farm. The father was worried to death and the mother was in hysterics.

Grandpa and the father and the twins' uncles walked to the edge of the farm to where a path went through the woods and into the swamp. They followed the path until it ended.

The father said, "They would have turned to the right here and headed back to high ground."

Grandpa asked, "Are they right-handed or left-handed?"

The father said, "Right-handed."

Grandpa knew that right handed people usually had a stronger right leg than left leg, and given no reference to keep them walking straight, would circle to the left as they walked.

So Grandpa searched to the left and the father and uncles searched to the right.

Grandpa followed instinct, and a hunch, and in an opening where the going was a little easier, he found a small fresh shoe print. And further on he found another fresh shoe print. And he tracked those boys way out into the swamp to where there wasn't much ground above water and it was all damp and boggy.

After a while Grandpa heard a little boy holler that he saw a light, and Grandpa went in that direction and he came up to the twins huddled by a huge cypress tree.

When Grandpa came up one twin hollered, "We're not lost." The other twin poked him in the ribs with his elbow and whispered, "You told me we were lost."

Grandpa said to the boys, "Looks like you men found a good campsite. I've been trying to find a good place like this to make camp tonight. With your permission I'll camp with you."

The boys said together, "Yes sir."

"We'll want a fire," Grandpa said. "You men get some dry limbs and twigs and we'll get one going."

"Yes sir," they said.

Grandpa proceeded to rub two hard dry sticks together, and in a few minutes he had a red hot place on the sticks, and he put some dry rotten wood dust on the hot place and blew gently on it and a little smoke came up. He blew some more and added some dry twigs and pretty soon he had a fire going. The boys' eyes were as big as saucers.

The boys had killed a big old swamp rabbit, and Grandpa said, "You men hungry?"

"Yes sir," they said.

Grandpa said, "We'll cook that fine big swamp rabbit if you want."

"Yes sir," they said.

Grandpa squeezed the rabbit with both hands and the entrails popped out the bottom. Then Grandpa packed wet mud from the creek bank all around the rabbit, skin, hair, head and all, until it looked like a giant mud ball. Then he scooted it up next to the fire and he told the boys, "I'll go get us some vegetables to eat with that rabbit. You know it's important to eat balanced meals. You men keep the fire going until I get back."

"Yes sir," they said.

Grandpa went back to where the father and the uncles were searching and said, "I've found the boys and they're fine."

"Well, where are they?" the father said.

Grandpa said, "We've got a campsite fixed up, and with your permission, we'll spend the night and hunt home in the morning."

"My wife would kill me," the father said.

Grandpa said, "You've got a hard job to do, but you need to go home and calm your misses down and explain to her that young boys have a fragile ego and you can kill their spirit by overreacting to every trial that they face. Mothers, by nature, would like to try to keep their children from growing up. But it is very important to let them grow as they need to. When the boys get home in the morning they'll be apologetic for the worry they caused. I'll explain it to them. So you all accept their apology and cut them some slack, please. And please call my wife and tell her I'll be camping out with the twins tonight."

The father said that he understood and he and the uncles headed back to the farm.

Grandpa pulled up some cattail roots on the way back to the camp. When he got there, the boys had the fire built up so high that they had to stand way back. They said that they wanted to be sure that Grandpa could find his way back.

Grandpa put the cattail roots in the coals next to the rabbit mud ball, and in a few minutes they were cooked.

Grandpa pulled the mud ball out of the coals and when it cooled down some, he cracked it open. Most of the hair came off in the dried mud. The rabbit was cooked well enough to eat, so Grandpa and the boys ate the rabbit and the cattail roots and washed it down with creek water. In those days you could drink out of a creek, but it is probably not a good idea now.

The boys said that it was the most delicious meal that they had ever tasted.

It's usually pretty chilly on Christmas night so Grandpa piled some leaves in between two big roots of the huge cypress to keep himself off of the wet ground, and he lay down to sleep with the fire reflecting warmth off of the big tree roots.

Before Grandpa lay down, he kneeled and said his prayers out loud. He said, "Big God, thank you for this beautiful swamp that supplies us with all these luxuries, like food, water, and the air we breathe. And thank you for giving us the knowledge that the only necessity in our lives is Salvation, which you provide for us, free for the asking. And thank you for providing a fine camping place, and such fine men and neighbors to camp with. And be with our loved ones at home, who we know are lonesome because we are not with them tonight. Forgive us our sins and guide us home safely tomorrow. In Jesus' name amen."

And both of the boys said, "Amen."

Then the boys lay down on the other side of the fire from Grandpa, but Grandpa said that when he woke up in the morning, they were piled up next to him, one on one side and one on the other side.

They hunted out the next morning, and when they got to the edge of the farm where the boys lived, Grandpa could tell that the boys wanted to break and run to their house, that they could see in the distance.

But one boy said in the huskiest voice that he could manage, "I guess we'll just hunt our way up to the house now. Maybe we can pick up a rabbit or two on the way."

The other boy said, "Yea."

Grandpa said, "If you men ever want to go camping in the swamp again, I'd be obliged if you'd let me tag along."

The boys stood up real straight and threw back their shoulders when Grandpa called them men. They said, "Yes sir."

Grandpa said, "When you get up to your house, you apologize to your mother for worrying her, and you promise to tell her where you're going from now on."

"Yes sir," they both said, and they started off toward their house. And they remembered to look all around like they were hunting.

Every year after that the twins came by on Christmas Day to get Grandpa to go roughing it, they called it, in the swamp for a night.

A few years after that on one Christmas Day Grandma told Grandpa, "The twins will be here to get you pretty soon."

Grandpa said, "Yea," and he said, "You know, I wish that back when all this got started years ago, that I had told those boys that it was all right to bring a sleeping bag when they go camping, and maybe bring some matches and some food."

The twins were in R.O.T.C. in college, and after college they went straight into the Army. They got in Special Forces and we heard they went behind enemy lines on special missions.

The VietNam war was going on when Grandpa died and we tried to reach the twins, but the military said that they couldn't get a message to them where they were.

After the war we saw the twins on the TV news. They had so many badges and medals on their uniforms that you couldn't have found room for another one. The TV reporter said that they were heroes.

When the twins retired from the military they came back around here to live, and they both have big Christian families now. And they are still important to the government and have to go to Washington, D.C. quite often.

Every Christmas somebody leaves something little on Grandpa's grave. It's always something from way out in the big swamp, like cattail roots, or the shed antler from an old swamp buck, or a swamp rabbit baked in mud.

And nobody ever sees who leaves it, except Grandpa.

Chapter Nine
The Murder

In the very early days, large animals traveled through the woods in their normal activities, and they usually followed the best or easiest route. Through centuries of use the animal routes became hard-packed trails. Early man also used these trails. European explorers in America followed the same trails, as did the first settlers. Eventually some trails were increased to wagon width and became roads. And today many of these early routes are modern highways.

The Old Swamp Road was a natural route through the piney woods and into the swamp, where it more or less ended at an old boat road through the flooded cypress area.

Just as the Old Swamp Road entered the swamp, it passed over a series of low sand hills that were the last high ground before the bottomland. Where the road went through the sand hills, it was in places worn down as much as ten feet deep from years of use and erosion.

These small hills were where the best squirrel hunting was. Both red fox squirrels and gray cat squirrels loved the mix of hardwood and pine trees on the swamp edge. On one of these sand hills, was where a squirrel hunter found human remains in a shallow grave that had been partly exposed by rooting hogs and erosion.

The squirrel hunter went straight to Grandpa and reported that he had found a dead man and he told Grandpa where it was. The squirrel hunter didn't want to go back anywhere around the vicinity of the dead man.

The squirrel hunter reported the dead man to Grandpa because Grandpa had sort of an informal agreement with the sheriff, that

Grandpa was the "law" in our corner of the parish, which was a long way from the parish seat where the sheriff stayed. Grandpa was kind of a vigilante at times.

So Grandpa went and investigated the dead man.

A few days later, the sheriff drove up to Grandpa's house, and over coffee served on the front porch, the sheriff asked Grandpa about the dead man. The sheriff had gotten word about the dead man being found and he wanted to know what Grandpa had found out.

The sheriff asked Grandpa, "Do you know how the man died?"

Grandpa said, "Yep, he was murdered."

The sheriff asked, "How was he murdered?"

Grandpa said, "He was shot and his throat was cut."

"What did you do with the evidence?" the sheriff asked.

"I dug the hole deeper and reburied him," Grandpa said.

The sheriff said, "You shouldn't have done that. We need the evidence. We can't have a murderer running loose around here."

Grandpa said, "You don't need to worry. The man who committed this murder is not running around here anymore. The murder was committed over five hundred years ago. The victim was shot in the pelvis with a flint tipped arrow. The flint arrowhead is still embedded in his pelvic bone. And, his throat was cut with a flint knife. The point of the flint knife is embedded in his neck vertebra. He was buried with pots and other grave goods, so I buried it all back deeper, so the pothunters couldn't find it. If you don't mind, don't let the story get out, or else we'll be invaded by pot hunters."

The sheriff said, "Okay, I won't let it out."

Two days later a truckload of men and boys with shovels and sifters drove up to Grandpa's house to ask directions to the Indian burial ground that the sheriff had told them about.

Where Grandpa told them to go, they didn't find any Indian graves or pots. Grandpa didn't believe in desecration of graves, even heathen graves.

Chapter Ten

The Guessing Game

Grandpa and Grandma had seven children: five boys and two girls. When they were all home, like in the summer when school was out, and the oldest was still not a teenager yet, Grandpa and Grandma reached a point where they needed private time to themselves, every once in a while.

So Grandpa devised a plan, called the Guessing Game. The game worked like this: Grandpa and Grandma would go for a walk, and when they got back, the kids would gather around them in the living room, and guess where Grandpa and Grandma had walked to based on clues that Grandpa and Grandma would provide. The winner of the game was, of course, the one who guessed correctly where Grandpa and Grandma had walked to.

The first day of the Guessing Game Grandpa and Grandma left and were gone for about an hour. When they returned, the kids gathered around and began guessing.

The oldest son, my uncle now, said, "By the red clay on Mama's shoes, I'm guessing that Mom and Dad walked down the old red clay road to the back forty today."

Grandpa said, "That is correct, son. You win the Guessing Game today."

The next time that Grandpa and Grandma played the Guessing Game they got back in about an hour and the kids gathered around for the guessing.

The oldest daughter said, "By the black mud on Mama's shoes, I'm guessing that Mom and Dad walked down the road to the edge of the big swamp today."

Grandpa said, "That is correct, sweetheart. You win the Guessing Game today."

The next time Grandpa and Grandma played the Guessing Game when they got back Grandma was carrying a pinecone.

The oldest son said, "I see the pinecone, but by the fact that Mama's hair is wet, I'm guessing that Mama and Dad went skinny dipping at the swimming hole today."

Grandma was always easy to blush and she started turning a little red. Grandpa had always taught the children to be truthful and he was always truthful himself. Grandpa said, "That is correct, son. You win the Guessing Game today."

The next time Grandpa and Grandma played the Guessing Game they were gone for about an hour and when they returned everybody gathered in the living room, and Grandma laid a handful of gravel on the side table.

The oldest son, ever suspicious of everything, said, "I see the gravel from the old gravel road, but because of the hay in Mama's hair, I'm guessing that Mama and Dad went to the hayloft in the barn today."

Grandma began to turn red again. Grandpa said, "That is correct, son. You win the Guessing Game today."

The next time that Grandpa and Grandma played the Guessing Game when they got back Grandma laid an ear of corn on the side table, then went straight to the bedroom. When she returned to the living room she was covered from head to foot with pink Calamine lotion.

The oldest son said, "I see the corn from the corn field, but judging by the Calamine lotion all over Mom, I'm guessing that Mama and Dad went to the poison ivy patch in the woods today."

The few parts of Grandma that weren't covered with Calamine lotion, turned red.

Grandpa said, "That is correct, son. You win the Guessing Game today. Now you kids can play the Guessing Game all you want among yourselves but your Mom and I have got to stop."

When Grandma died and then the next year Grandpa died, it

threw a bad gloom on everybody.

On the day of Grandpa's funeral, after the funeral, all the relatives went back to Grandpa and Grandma's house. Ladies from the church had brought lots of food and it was set out in the dining room and in the living room.

But nobody felt like eating. Nobody was talking.

Then my oldest uncle said, "I'm guessing that Mom and Dad went to Heaven today."

My uncles and aunts looked at each other. In their minds they could hear Grandpa say, "That is correct, son. You win the Guessing Game today."

My youngest aunt started laughing, and my other aunt and my uncles started laughing. And they laughed until some of them were rolling on the floor.

When they finally stopped laughing, the gloom was gone. It was like Grandpa and Grandma had sent a message from the grave to mend their broken hearts.

Everybody was happy now. And the food from the church didn't last long after that.

One thing is not a guess. It is certain: Grandpa and Grandma are truly in Heaven today.

Chapter Eleven

Skunk Ape

Since early days, even since Indian times, there have been reports of a large, strange, humanlike animal in the Big Swamp. It is the Louisiana version of Big Foot and Abominable Snowman rolled into one.

This shy, unusual creature lives in the swamp and is rarely seen by humans. Reports from people who have seen the creature always emphasize the strong, bad smell that it gives off. The bad odor is the reason that the animal is called the skunk ape.

A team of scientists from the State University came to Grandpa for help in locating the skunk ape for research they were doing. They wanted pictures and a live specimen if possible. The scientists had been informed that Grandpa was the best authority on the Big Swamp, and that he would be the best person to guide them to the skunk ape.

The scientists interviewed Grandpa, and he told them that he had never actually seen a skunk ape, but he had smelled them several times.

Grandpa agreed to take them to the most probable skunk ape location, and he told them that it would be a difficult trip.

Grandpa and the scientists got their gear together and headed out into the swamp. They penetrated into the interior of the swamp as far as they could go without getting closer to the other side. Grandpa found some semisolid ground, and they set up a camp. It was the dry season, but even so, it was necessary to support the camp with poles and brush laid on the mud.

Once the camp was established, Grandpa began to scout for

skunk ape sign.

On the third day out, Grandpa located some huge tracks in the mud. He took the scientists to the tracks and they excitedly made pictures and measurements. They all commented on the strange, bad odor in the vicinity of the tracks. The tracks couldn't be followed or back trailed because of deeper water.

The scientists decided to build a blind, or hide, so one of them could stay and watch in case the skunk ape came back. So one of them stayed in the blind and the others went back to the camp with Grandpa.

After supper, at the time they usually turned in for the night, Grandpa told the others that he was a little worried about the man in the blind, and that he thought he better go check on him.

The others said, "Okay," and Grandpa went to check.

Grandpa had not been gone from the camp very long when the scientists noticed a very bad odor drifting into the camp from the surrounding swamp. They got real quite and then they could hear some low grunts and growls. Then the growls got louder, and the smell got so bad that they could hardly stand it. Then they saw a dark manlike figure walking on two legs just at the edge of the campfire light.

The scientists piled all of the firewood on the fire, and they screamed and hollered as loud as they could until the beast left. Then they huddled as close as they could get to the fire.

The same thing happened to the scientist in the blind, only he didn't have a fire. Luckily, Grandpa heard him screaming and made it to the blind before anything bad happened to the man.

Grandpa took the scientist back to the camp and listened while the terrified scientists told what had happened.

The head scientist told Grandpa, "We've got all the information on the skunk ape that we need. You take us out of here first thing in the morning!"

Grandpa said, "I took this job to earn enough money to pay for a new heating unit for the church and I'm not leaving until I've earned that much."

The scientist said, "How much does the heating unit cost?"
Grandpa told him the amount.

The scientist said, "I calculate that you will have earned that exact amount by the time we get home tomorrow."

So they left the swamp the next morning, the scientists paid Grandpa, and went back to the University where they wrote a big report to justify the skunk ape grant that they had received.

They concluded that the skunk ape was a primitive, manlike being that lived in the swamp, smelled really bad, and was very dangerous and should be left alone from now on.

The Church enjoyed the new heating unit.

Grandma said that when she was unpacking Grandpa's camping stuff, his huge bottle of home-made buck lure fell out of his pack. She said that even with the top on the bottle, she could barely stand the smell.

A couple of months later the scientists sent Grandpa a copy of their final report. In the report were pictures that the man in the blind had made with his night camera.

Grandma said that apparently, skunk apes have a strong resemblance to Grandpa.

Chapter Twelve

The Horse Race

Grandpa didn't ride horses for pleasure, but he always kept one or two around his place for the kids and the grandkids to ride. And sometimes he rode a horse to round up his woods cows, or to bring in a deer that he had killed way back in the woods.

Years ago Grandpa bought a young quarter horse colt which grew up to become a very special horse. It was fast.

The quarter horse breed was developed mostly from Thoroughbred bloodlines with enough other blood to make them tough for ranch work and so forth. Thoroughbred racehorses were developed to race distances of a mile or more, on an oval track. Quarter horses were developed to run one quarter of a mile down a straight track, usually in a matched race with one other horse.

Whereas Thoroughbred horses are tall and equally powerful all over, quarter horses are more compact, and have powerful hindquarters, developed for acceleration, like a sprinter.

Quarter horse racing is very popular in Louisiana and our State Senator at the time was a quarter horse breeder and racer. And he was quite a fanatic about it.

The Senator heard about Grandpa's horse, and tried to buy it.

But Grandpa said, "No thank you."

Every time that the Senator ran into Grandpa anywhere he would ask Grandpa to sell the horse, and Grandpa would say, "No thank you."

Finally the Senator encountered Grandpa at the State Champion baseball game where their school played ours, and in front of a crowd the Senator challenged Grandpa to a match race, winner take both horses.

Now Grandpa didn't gamble, but he also didn't suffer fools lightly, so he answered the challenge like this:

Grandpa said, "I'll race you under two conditions.

First: I don't want your horse, so if you lose, you'll paint our church house.

Second: The starting point will be on the road where my driveway turns off. I'll mark the finish line exactly one quarter of a mile away."

They settled on a date and time, and shook hands.

On the agreed date and time, Grandpa was waiting at the driveway gate when the Senator arrived. Grandpa had the bridle reins of his horse looped around the gate. His old western saddle was on the horse's back. His horse wasn't even shod (it didn't have horseshoes on).

The Senator opened his horse trailer door and unloaded his beautiful racehorse. The Senator's jockey oversaw while the Senator's groom saddled the powerful horse, which had never been beaten in a race. They had the latest style racing saddle and bridle.

When the preliminaries were over, the Senator looked up and down the road and asked Grandpa where the finish line was, so that he could send his entourage on ahead to judge the finish.

Grandpa pointed south and said, "The finish line is at the front gate of the Jones place, exactly one quarter of a mile straight across Boggy Creek bottom. The nearest bridge is ten miles up the road that way." And he pointed east.

The Senator wasn't stupid and he knew Grandpa could cross Boggy Bottom in a hurry leading his woods horse. And he knew that the fancy racehorse would never make it across and the bridge was much too far away.

The Senator said, "Load the horse boys. We've been had."

The Senator was a politician and he knew people so he turned to Grandpa and said. "Show me where your church house is and what color you want it painted."

And the Senator and his men did a good job on the church house and it got the Senator a lot of votes.

The preacher objected to the church house being painted as a result of gambling, but Grandpa reminded him, that it's only gambling if there's a chance that you might lose.

Grandpa said, "There was never any chance of me losing that horse race."

Chapter Thirteen
The Vote

Grandpa and Grandma had six children when Baby came along. All of the children became hunters when they were old enough. Grandpa and Grandma's rule was, that to go on a real hunting trip, the child must be at least ten years old, and must be proficient and safe with a gun, plus other things like making good grades in school, and so forth.

Grandpa and Grandma would be considered very strict in this day and time and they ruled their home with an iron hand, so to speak.

Grandpa was fond of saying, "You don't let the inmates run the asylum."

It was a 'big deal' to get to go to the deer camp with Grandpa for the opening day of deer season. And whether you got a deer or not, being part of the family at the deer camp was a very important tradition.

The kids, and Grandpa too, spent many hours plotting and planning and preparing their gear for the big day. The deer rifles were all checked to make sure that the sights were perfectly on target.

Baby got her gear ready and her rifle sighted in, and proclaimed that she was ready for her first hunt. But Grandpa and Grandma told her that she couldn't go yet because she was only nine and a half year's old.

Baby was heartbroken. She knew all the safety rules and she could hit the vital area of the deer target every time with her rifle. And she was almost ten years old.

On the afternoon of the day before deer season opened, Grandpa loaded his gear into the truck, and called for the kids to load their gear and get in. The kids had everything piled on the front porch, ready to load.

But the oldest boy, always a rebel, said, "I believe that Baby is old enough to start hunting with us and I won't go if she can't go. I'll stay with Baby."

And each other child in turn, said, "I'll stay with Baby." And many tears flowed, including Grandpa's and Grandma's.

Grandpa kissed and hugged Baby and each other child in turn, and he kissed and hugged Grandma, and then drove off alone. Because even if all of the inmates vote to do something, they still don't run the asylum.

Chapter Fourteen
The Church

Our little church was organized over one hundred and fifty years ago. One of our local pioneer families donated one acre of land to be used for a church and one acre to be used as a cemetery.

The first church building was made of logs. The second building was made of lumber. The present building is made of brick.

The church was organized as a Denomination. The little church was well attended, but being a rural church in a sparsely populated area the membership was never large.

As was customary, the services were quiet and reserved. The preacher never raised his voice, and nary a sound was ever heard from the congregation. Even the singing was quiet and reserved. Eventually an organ replaced the old piano, and it was played in a quiet and reserved manner.

The sermons were usually about all the different ways you could get sent to Hell. And it seemed like most of the congregation were there because they thought they had to be there, not because they wanted to be there. And, no doubt, many Christians passed through our old church on their way to Heaven.

Then one Sunday about fifty years ago, a strange thing happened. The congregation was in church service, just praying quietly, when they heard a loud noise. Some witnesses said it was a scream. Some said it was a loud horn blowing. Some said it was thunder. Grandpa said it was a loud wind like a forest fire makes.

Then what the witnesses said they saw gets confused. Some witnesses say that they saw Grandpa get in a fight. Some say that he threw a man down. Some witnesses say that Grandpa hit a man with his fist and knocked him down and then threw him out of the church and locked the door.

Grandpa said that he don't remember any fight. That all he remembers is praying real hard.

Grandma said that Grandpa's knuckles were all skinned up, and his hands were blistered like they were burnt from whatever had happened.

Anyway, somebody in the congregation shouted, "Hallelujah!"

And somebody shouted, "Praise God!"

Then everybody started worshiping and praising God in a real devoted and emotional way, and there was a lot of confusion.

The preacher usually kept track of the time, and at exactly twelve o'clock noon he would dismiss the church because the people wanted to get home to eat dinner. But he didn't dismiss at twelve o'clock this day because everybody was worshiping and praising God, and nobody wanted to leave.

Finally, after hours went by, the people started going home. They were all happy and hugging each other and some were crying.

The church Board of Directors met and some of them were wringing their hands and worrying. One of them said, "The Denomination is going to kick us out when they find out what has happened to our church."

Grandpa was on the board. He said, "Everybody has a choice. They can obey God, or they can obey the Denomination. As for me and my house, we will serve the Lord."

And the people continued to worship and praise God in their new way. And their outward appearance changed as they began to worship more. The men got men's haircuts, shaved, and wore men's clothes. And the women let their hair grow and they wore only women's clothes, and they did away with makeup and jewelry. And low and behold, they were beautiful.

But the main thing that changed was their attitude. Now instead of church being something they had to do, church became what they wanted to do most of all. And the preacher, instead of preaching quietly behind the lectern, used every inch of the platform and a lot of the aisles too, in very emotional worshiping and praise of God. And the choir sang so loud that they had to turn the volume down instead of up. And the old organ couldn't keep up, so they got a keyboard, and drums, and cymbals, and horns, and they made a joyful noise unto the Lord.

Our people still get old and die and we miss them when they're gone. But we don't worry about them, because we know that they have gone to a better place.

And the Denomination didn't have to kick us out. We resigned. Now we call ourselves Pentecostal.

Chapter Fifteen
Angel

Grandpa and Grandma's kids were all either well along in school or already out on their own when Angel came along. Grandma thought that at near fifty years old she wouldn't have any more children, but God is good, and he blessed Grandpa and Grandma with Angel.

Angel came a little early and was small at birth, but she did well under Grandma's loving care.

The girls and women in our family are known for great beauty as well as brains and athletic ability. But Angel looked a little different and she learned to walk late, and was a little clumsy.

Angel didn't do well in the first grade, so Grandma talked to the teacher and agreed to teach Angel at home. Angel learned well for Grandma. She was Grandma's constant companion and was a joy to both Grandpa and Grandma.

As each different kind of wildflower bloomed in the spring and through the year, Angel would pick some and put them in a Mason jar, and place them around the house for Grandma to see. And Grandma would always make a big fuss about how beautiful they were.

And Angel would always say, "You know what I want Grandma?"

And Grandma would say, "What do you want, Angel?"

And Angel would say, "I want to be beautiful."

And Grandma would always say, "You are beautiful, Angel."

When Angel was seventeen, God needed another beautiful Angel in heaven and He called Angel. And she went.

There was lots of grief and tears at Grandpa's and Grandma's. But even though they didn't understand God's Plan, they knew that He had a Plan, and that it was good.

In the spring and throughout the year, Grandma would pick each different kind of wildflower as they bloomed and put them in a Mason jar and place it by Angel's grave.

And on Angel's headstone, Grandma had them write, "Angel Is Beautiful."

Chapter Sixteen
Brad P.

Grandpa and Grandma had a big family. Lots of kids, and when they all finally left the nest, Grandpa and Grandma had a little touch of the Empty Nest Syndrome.

One Sunday when they got to the church there was a crowd gathered around something on the church steps. Everybody was looking at a little urchin boy. He was dirty and barefoot and had rags for clothes.

Grandma reached for the boy but he drew back like he thought he was going to get hit.

Grandma said, "What's your name, son?"

The boy said, "I reckon it's Brat. That's all I've ever been called."

"Are you hungry, Brad?" Grandma said. His pronunciation was so bad that she thought he said his name was Brad.

"Yea," he said.

"Where's your mama?" Grandma asked.

"She's gone. She told me not to try to follow her no more," Brad said.

"Where's your dad?" Grandma asked.

"Never had no dad," Brad said.

The church Elders said, "We'll have to send this boy into town and let the government put him in an orphanage for his own good because nobody will take him."

Grandpa looked at Grandma and she nodded.

And Grandpa said, "We'll take him."

Grandpa and Grandma took Brad home, and into their home. They tried to give Brad a bath, but he had never had a bath and he fought it. So Grandpa asked Brad if he would like to go swimming, and Brad said, "Yes."

So Brad and Grandpa went to the swimming hole and swam. Grandma sent some of the other kids' outgrown clothes along and after the swim, Brad put the new-to-him clothes on. He was so proud. They were the first good clothes that he had ever had, and the first underwear. It would be a while before Brad would tolerate shoes.

Brad's skinny little body was covered with scars and sores, but Grandma knew just what to treat them with and Brad began to heal on the outside. And with Grandma's special hugs, Brad began to heal on the inside. He had a long way to go.

One time Grandma asked Brad if he wanted Grandpa to try and find his mother.

Brad said, "No. My mama is the meanest person in the world."

Brad used a lot of profanity. He didn't know the words were bad. It was part of his language.

Slowly, Grandpa and Grandma taught him which words were good and which were bad, and that if a person used bad words people wouldn't like and respect him.

Grandma taught Brad how to eat with a fork and spoon and knife. And she taught him table manners.

At first Brad stole food and hid it in his room. But as he began to fatten up, he began to realize that he didn't need to steal food, that Grandma would always provide meals at regular mealtimes.

And Brad's spindly little bowlegs caused by rickets and malnutrition, started to straighten up. And his dark hair grew in thick and shiny.

Grandma said that Brad "cleaned up" real nice.

Brad had very little sense of right or wrong and no sense at all of privacy or personal property rights. But Grandpa and Grandma had lots of patience, and slowly Brad learned what was right.

Brad still couldn't abide shoes, so Grandpa made him a pair of Indian moccasins and told him how Indians wore them hunting and how silently they could slip through the woods. So Brad tried moccasins and found that he liked them.

Grandma and Grandpa always took Brad to church with them and they explained how Jesus could erase bitterness, forgive sins, and give salvation. And they taught Brad how to pray.

When it came time for Brad to start school in the first grade he was well prepared. And his conduct was good. And Grandma and Grandpa were proud, because they loved Brad and he loved them.

When Brad came home from his first day at school, he told Grandma that he needed another name. That all the other kids had two names, like Bobbie Ann, or Bernice Ray, or Randy Bill, or Booker T.

So Grandma told Brad to pick another name and he picked P because it sounded good. So from then on Brad was known as Brad P.

By high school time, Brad P was easily considered the best looking boy in school. And he was certainly better looking than any of the boys and men in our family. Our men were never called handsome. Rugged maybe, but never handsome.

But Brad P was handsome. He was well built, and had wavy black hair, and a dark complexion, like a good suntan.

And Brad P was smart. He finished school in the top of his class. Then he studied under our pastor, to be an evangelist. And one day it came time for Brad P to hit the evangelism trail.

Brad P packed his bags and said his goodbyes to Grandpa and Grandma, and there was a lot of crying, from both happiness and sadness.

Brad P hugged and kissed Grandma, then he hugged Grandpa, then he shook Grandpa's hand.

And he said to Grandpa, "Sir, you've been more than a father to me and I'll never forget it. I've never had a last name, but with your permission, I'd like to take your name as my last name."

Grandpa said through tears, "I'd be honored."

So Brad P left home, and on his way he went through the Parish Seat, and stopped at the courthouse and had his new last name legally registered.

Brad P went all over the United States evangelizing, and he was much in demand.

Several years later our pastor asked Brad P to lead a revival at our church, and he accepted.

I've never seen Grandpa more proud than on the first day of the revival when he and Grandma walked around the corner at the church, and first saw the big sign outside the church.

The sign read, "Starting Monday, Weeklong revival, Lead by Evangelist Brad P Grandpa.

Chapter Seventeen

Firewood

Every spring, before the summer heat set in, Grandpa would cut firewood (he called it farwood) to replace what he had burned during the winter.

Grandpa and Grandma heated their house with a fireplace for as long as they could manage it. They liked the warmth and the atmosphere that a fireplace fire created.

Grandpa and Grandma often ate their meals in front of the fireplace in the winter. They loved to sit there in the evening and soak up the warm rays that radiated from the friendly fire. Grandpa said that man has been warmed by fire for thousands of years, and that warming by a fire is a natural thing to do. Grandpa said that you could learn more sitting and staring into a fire, than you could learn sitting and staring at a television set.

As Grandpa and Grandma got older, we encouraged them to get central heating so that they wouldn't have to struggle with firewood each year.

Grandpa said that as long as Grandma could load it, he could cut it. So every spring they went firewood cutting on the back side of their property. Grandpa would hitch the trailer to the old farm tractor and they would go get a tree here and there, as they chose.

Grandpa liked cherry bark oak the best, and hickory second best, but he would cut a white oak if it got in his way. The heaviest wood burns the longest and gives the most heat. The softer, lighter woods like pine, maple, and gum, burn too fast and make a lot of ash. Green and white ash make good stove wood, but Grandpa usually didn't cut ash for the fireplace.

Grandpa would also get rich lightered pine; he called it fat pine, to start the fires with. There were lots of fat pine stumps remaining from the huge virgin pines that were cut many years before.

Grandpa cut the trees down and into firewood lengths with his chainsaw. Grandma toted the wood and loaded it on the trailer. Grandma was surprisingly strong for such a sweet and gentle woman.

Grandma could load all but the largest firewood sticks by herself. She and Grandpa lifted together on the big sticks that neither one of them could have loaded alone.

Grandma refused to wear gloves until the day she was swinging an extra heavy stick into the trailer and didn't quite clear the angel iron rail. The weight of the heavy stick caught the tip of her finger between the stick and the rail, and mashed it pretty hard.

Grandma never used profanity and she fussed if anyone said dang or darn. But Grandpa said that she said plenty of dangs and darns, and asked God to bless her finger on that day. He said that she hopped around like a wild Indian doing a war dance.

After Grandma's fingernail grew back she would wear gloves, but she didn't like to.

Grandpa used to love to split firewood with a maul. He said that it was therapeutic and didn't take any brains. But he said that about hoeing in the garden and several other things that looked like work to us kids. Most of us had read *Tom Sawyer*, and we were on the lookout for such as that. But in later years Grandpa's shoulder joint wouldn't hold up to splitting with a maul, so he rigged up a homemade firewood splitter that worked pretty well.

A salesman from the gas company came around to Grandpa's trying to sell central heating units. He told Grandpa that a fireplace actually sucked more heat out of the house than it created.

Grandpa said that he wished the pioneers would have known that. He said it would have saved a lot of trees.

There finally came a day when Grandpa and Grandma couldn't handle the fireplace anymore. Even with our help, the fireplace was too much trouble for them, and even dangerous, we thought.

So Grandpa and Grandma got a central heating unit installed in their house and everybody was happy about it. Except Grandpa. He said that it just wasn't natural to back up and try to warm your behind in a stream of hot air coming out of a hole in the ceiling.

Chapter Eighteen
Hog Wild

Back in Grandpa's younger days there was no law against loose stock (farm animals) in Louisiana.

Lots of small farmers let their stock, especially hogs, run loose most of the time. The farmers identified their stock with brands, or in the case of hogs, with marks cut into the hogs' ears.

These marks were recorded at the courthouse, and in general, people recognized ownership of loose stock by the marks that they carried.

Hog ear marks were usually a combination of notches on one ear or both ears. Sometimes the ear was cut square across the top and the notches were cut in the remaining half.

Grandpa's registered mark was a deep narrow notch that went from the center of the tip of each ear, to the center of the base of each ear. It was called the four-ear mark because it made the hog look like it had four ears, two on each side of the head.

Farmers usually had a hog dog that would catch loose hogs so that the farmer could mark the unmarked young hogs and neuter the young male hogs. The hogs became very wild while living loose, and hog hunting was considered to be very exciting and dangerous to man and dog.

Un-neutered male hogs, called boars, would usually develop long tusks. The tusks would be very sharp, because the lower tusks rubbed against the upper ones and were continuously sharpened. The female hogs, called sows, also had razor sharp tusks that were usually shorter than boar tusks, but were equally deadly.

Both boars and sows could be very dangerous when cornered, and sows were particularly protective when they had young, which was most of the time.

Most of the hogs were black or red. Some were white, and a few were spotted. Occasionally some had a white band over the shoulders like the Hampshire breed has.

Grandpa favored spotted hogs, so he always left a spotted boar un-neutered. As a result most of Grandpa's hogs were spotted.

During the dry season of the year, Grandpa's hogs would travel south, down the edge of the big swamp, looking for food. Hogs will eat just about anything, and can find food when most wildlife can't.

Occasionally Grandpa's hogs would forage so far south that they crossed the parish line into the neighboring parish below us. This parish to the south of us has had a bad reputation ever since they seceded from Louisiana in the War Between the States.

Civil War deserters and other undesirable characters migrated to that parish for refuge from the authorities. The bad element elected one of their own as Sheriff, and as District Attorney, and as Judge, and to most of the other elected offices in the parish.

Gangs of robbers controlled the roads through the parish and would attack, rob, and kill travelers through the parish. They even attacked and robbed military payroll details.

For years after the Civil War, and even into the twentieth century, the corruption persisted. Even today, the bad reputation persists in that parish.

On one occasion Grandpa trailed his hogs all the way into that parish south of us and found his hogs in a pen at the rundown farm of a notorious hog thief.

Grandpa recognized his hogs even though his mark had been changed to the no-ears mark that was registered to the hog thief.

It is obvious to any reasonable person that the no-ears mark was just a convenient way to get rid of the previous owner's mark.

Sometimes an aggressive hog dog would pull the ear off of a hog, but that left a scar that was different from the scar left by a sharp knife.

In most parishes, the no-ears mark would not be allowed as a registered mark, but in the bad parish it was approved.

Grandpa took his pickup truck with a cattle frame on the back to the hog thief's rundown farm and started loading the hogs into his truck to bring them home. Before Grandpa got the first load loaded, the crooked sheriff showed up and charged Grandpa with stealing hogs. A court date was set to hear the case before the corrupt judge.

On the court day Grandpa appeared at the courthouse without a lawyer, and was seated at the defendant's table. The trial started and the crooked prosecutor called the hog thief to the witness stand. The hog thief testified that the hogs were his and that the proof was that they all had his no-ears mark.

The crooked sheriff testified that he caught Grandpa in the act of stealing the hogs from the hog thief's pen. The prosecution rested its case, and the judge called for the defense.

Grandpa stood up and went to the front before the judge.

Grandpa said, "Those spotted hogs are mine. They had my four-ears mark, which was cut off to form the no-ears mark. That it happened is obvious, but I can't prove it. Instead, I've brought five character witnesses." Grandpa pointed to the first row of spectators. "That big man on the end is the High Sheriff of our parish. The next man is our District Judge. The next man is the pastor of our church. The next man is the State Representative, who is from our parish, and the fifth man is a State Senator, who is also from our parish. These five men don't know much about hogs, but they know me well. They came to testify of one thing: that if I say I'm going to do something, then I'm going to do it, period."

Grandpa pointed to my Dad and my four uncles who were sitting on the second row. The five men filled up the whole row. A couple of them were so big that they took up two seats. And there wasn't an once of fat amongst them. They weren't handsome men, and they didn't have on fine clothes. They just sat there, quite and serious-like.

Grandpa continued, "Those five men are my sons. Let me say this real delicately so that no one will take it as a threat. They are going to help me load up my spotted hogs and take them home." And

Grandpa sat back down.

The corrupt judge got blood red in the face. He looked at the crooked sheriff, and he looked at the crooked prosecutor. They both were a little pale. The judge looked at each of Grandpa's character witnesses, and at each of Grandpa's big sons.

The crooked judge rapped two times with his gavel, and then he said, "I'm dismissing this case due to lack of evidence." Then the judge pointed at the hog thief and said, "Don't you ever touch another spotted hog."

Grandpa and my Dad and my uncles loaded up Grandpa's spotted hogs and brought them back to Grandpa's hog pen. It took several loads to bring them all back. Just to be sure, Grandpa branded them all on the hip with a homemade branding iron that made a brand shaped like four ears.

Grandpa never lost any more hogs to the parish to our south.

Something unusual and sort of related, I guess, happened around about that time and for years afterward. Every once in a while, somebody in our area would kill a deer with four cars.

But, nobody in the parish south of us ever reported killing anything with the four-ear mark.

Chapter Nineteen
The Sheep

My brother was a good student and a good athlete in school. He loved to hunt and he went to church regularly like we all did. Everybody liked him and he had lots of friends. He was my hero. Brother graduated from college and then went into the army.

We were so happy when Brother finally came home to stay. But Brother had changed. He didn't go hunting anymore and he didn't go to church.

He had a good job and bought a house, and he lived in it by himself. After a while he quit coming to see us. We didn't know why.

Then he got put in jail. And nobody talked about Brother. It was like he didn't exist. Except for Grandpa. Every time Grandpa said the blessing at mealtime, he thanked God for Brother and asked God to place guardian angels around him.

Then Brother lost his job and he lost his house. And the only time Brother wasn't drunk was when he was in jail. And every night and morning Grandpa got on his knees and prayed to God to be with my brother. And all the rest of us did, too.

Nobody in town liked my brother or respected him anymore. They called him the "Black Sheep".

Brother finally hit bottom. And he almost died from alcohol abuse.

One Sunday he staggered into our little church and started to make a scene. But the Big Shepherd said, "Devil, you've tortured my sheep long enough." And God chased the Devil out of my brother. And my brother fell down on the altar and asked God to forgive him, and God did. And my brother began to heal. And by the Grace of

God, Brother went from the very bottom to the very top.

Brother is well-respected now. He is a good Christian, and he has a good Christian wife, and good Christian kids. And they go hunting with Grandpa every chance they get.

And, I think Grandpa is more proud of Brother than anybody else I know.

Chapter Twenty
Tough Love

Grandpa didn't like going places very much. Unless it was hunting. But Grandma liked to go to the State Fair every year and ride the rides and lose money at the booths.

So every year at fair time they went to the Fair in their old truck. It was a three-hour drive, but Grandma liked to drive, so off they went. And I got to go with them one year.

The only thing that Grandpa liked to do at the Fair was look at the animals. He said that he read that they had a thousand-pound hog there and he wanted to see it.

So we went into the old dark animal barn and it looked like we were the only people at the Fair that wanted to see the pigs. When we got back to the far end of the barn there were three men there. The one in front was the biggest, meanest looking, monster of a man that I had ever seen.

They blocked our way and that huge, mean man told Grandpa, "We won't kill you if you give us all your money." They had their hands bulging in their pockets like they had weapons.

What happened next happened so fast that I didn't know if I really saw it happen.

Now, Grandpa wasn't real old in those days and he was in good shape from hard work. His hands were as hard as wood, and he had long arms and big wrists.

Grandpa took a step forward and hit that monster man in the middle of his chest, just at the bottom of his rib cage, and Grandpa's fist almost disappeared in that guy's stomach. I heard ribs busting like somebody splitting kindling. The ground shook when that big man hit the floor, and he lay there curled up in a ball and he couldn't get his breath. The other two hoodlums started backing up but they couldn't get away because of the hog stalls. They jerked their hands out of their pockets and held them up to show that they were empty. By now they could see the pistol Grandpa was wearing on his belt. He had a permit from the Sheriff to carry it concealed.

One of the two men managed to stammer out, "What you gonna do now?"

Grandpa said, "Tell the big man that if he'll come to our church next Sunday, I'll help him find a job."

"Yes sir," they both said, and Grandpa told them where our church was, and we left.

That big monster man was still curled up on the floor.

The next Sunday a big, huge man came into our church during service and sat on the back pew next to the door. He had tape wrapped round and round his body over his ribs.

At the end of the service, during the altar call; everybody went up front except Grandpa. He went to the back and sat by the big man.

On Monday Grandpa called somebody at the mill, and from then on the big man met every shift and waited, and if somebody didn't show up he'd get to work that shift.

In a few months a permanent opening came up at the mill and they hired the big man on full time because he was a hard worker and smart. At the mill they nicknamed him Moose, because everybody said he was the biggest guy they had ever seen.

One year something went bad wrong in the mill and there was a big explosion and fire, and it cut off a bunch of workers in the back. Neighbors said you could hear the concussion twenty-six miles away.

Moose was working in the mill yard at the time of the explosion. He went into the mill through a fiery hole in the wall, and everybody knew he'd be killed, but he came back out dragging one man in each hand by the back of their shirt necks. Then he went in again and got two more, then again, then again.

Finally the fire trucks and rescue trucks got there, and the rescue people had on Nemex suits and air tanks, but it was too bad to go in any more. They ganged up on Moose and kept him from going back in again.

But everybody was out anyway. Some of them were in pretty bad shape, but they all lived. For years after that, they all used to brag about who had the biggest scars and scrape marks from where Moose dragged them through the rubble and up and down the stairs.

Moose wasn't the same color on the outside as me and Grandpa and most of the other people in our parish, but I bet that if he had run for president of the United States, he would have gotten every vote in our parish and the surrounding parishes, too.

Moose was a pallbearer at Grandpa's funeral, and he cried like a baby through the whole thing.

It's a terrible thing to see a big man cry. Then again, sometimes it's not.

Chapter Twenty-One
The Doctor

When I was a kid, we had an old camp house on our property. It was located right where the pine uplands ended and the pin oak (water/willow oak) flats began.

Grandpa built the camp house many years ago, out of cypress slabs left over from a small logging and portable sawmill operation in the big swamp. It was a small one-room cabin with built-in bunks, and a wood burning stove for cooking and heating.

We didn't use the cabin very much because we lived close to the good hunting. But every once in a while, some of our out-of-town relatives or friends would come to hunt and stay for a night or two in the cabin.

One of these friends was a medical doctor from New Orleans. I only saw him once. I was very young at the time, and hadn't ever been on a real hunting trip before, when one spring, on the day before turkey season opened, a big, black car drove up to our house.

The driver got out and came up to our front porch. Mama had heard the car come up, and she met the driver at the door and asked him if he would like to come in. The driver said no thank you, that he was here to pick up the boy, who Grandpa had arranged to help the Doctor at the hunting camp, for the turkey hunt.

Mom didn't look too happy about the plans, but she had agreed with Grandpa to let me go. I had my woods clothes packed and ready.

I tried to shake hands goodbye with Mom, but she kissed and hugged me anyway, right in front of the stranger. She told me to be careful as we walked to the car.

The driver put my bag in the turtle hull (car trunk) and opened the back car door for me to get in.

I had never ridden in a car before. Around our part of Louisiana at that time, everybody who had a vehicle had a pick-up truck.

As I got into the car, I saw that there was a big, tall man sitting on the other side in the back. He had snow-white hair. The driver introduced him as the Doctor.

I found out later, that a long time ago, Grandpa had taken Grandma to the big hospital in New Orleans and that the Doctor, through God, had helped her through a serious sickness. A friendship had developed between the Doctor and Grandpa, and ever since the Doctor would visit for a turkey hunt when his duties permitted.

It was a short drive to the camp. The big car handled the rough road pretty well. When we arrived at the camp, the driver came around and opened the car door for the Doctor. The Doctor got out and placed his hand on the driver's shoulder and they walked to the cabin. I figured from that, that the Doctor either couldn't walk too well or had bad eyesight.

The cabin was spotless inside. Grandpa, or somebody, had cleaned it up and put out fresh bedding. And stacked kindling and firewood by the wood stove and stocked the shelves with canned and boxed food. The cedar water barrel was filled with fresh water. The Doctor moved around in the cabin like he knew where everything would be.

It was getting dark by then, so the driver lit the coal oil lamp and then he unloaded the trunk of the car and brought our stuff into the cabin. The Doctor had a small bag of hunting clothes and a hand-tooled leather gun case with his gun in it.

I had had an early supper at home and really didn't need anything else to eat.

The driver got out some sandwiches that they had brought, and we all sat around a little fire in front of the cabin. We sat in the Adirondack style chairs that Grandpa had made out of cypress slabs.

Even with no cushion in the chair, I must have fallen asleep pretty early. I took after Grandpa in my sleeping habits. When it got dark in the evening, I got sleepy, and when it started to get light in the morning I got wide-awake.

When I woke up, well before daylight, I was in my bunk in the cabin. I suppose that the driver or the Doctor must have carried me in. I didn't remember anything.

The Doctor was already up cooking grits and coffee on the wood stove. It smelled real good, and I was hungry.

The Doctor blessed the food, and we sat at the makeshift table and ate while the driver slept on. He was a medium-loud snorer, and very steady at it.

The grits looked like Mom's, but when I took the first bite, I almost spit it out. Tears came to my eyes there was so much black pepper in those grits. Mom's were always sort of bland, with a little butter on top. But I ate the whole bowl, and pretended not to notice.

Grandpa was known for making strong coffee, but one cup of the Doctor's coffee would have made a gallon of Grandpa's, and it would have made ten gallons of Mom's.

After breakfast, we dressed in our hunting clothes and were ready to go before the sky started pinking.

The plan, as explained to me by Grandpa every day for the last week, was for me to take the Doctor to the big pin oak flat where the turkeys usually gathered when they left their roost first thing most mornings.

I was very young, seven years old as I remember, but I had grown up following Grandpa around this place, and I knew where to go.

Before we left the cabin, the Doctor opened his beautiful hand-tooled leather gun case and took out the most beautiful shotgun that I had never even imagined existed.

The shotgun had two barrels like Grandpa's and my Dad's, but instead of the barrels being side by side, one barrel was above and one was below. The gun was covered with beautiful engraving, and there were hunting scenes inlaid in gold on the flat sides above the trigger.

The wood in the stock and fore-end was the darkest black walnut that I had ever seen. And the grain in the walnut went round and round, instead of straight. It looked more like marble than like wood.

The Doctor put his hand on my shoulder, and we went by the best route to the edge of the big pin oak flat, where we settled down behind some low brush to wait for the turkeys.

It wasn't long before dawn started creeping in. We heard a hoot owl in the swamp, hoot eight times. They always hoot eight times. Never seven, never nine, always eight. They go: hoot-hoot, hoot-hoot; hoot-hoot, hoot-hoooo.

Exactly as soon as the hoot ended, the loudest, most awful gobble let out in the pines near us. It raised me off the ground a foot or two, I think. Then we heard some dry limbs breaking, and the sound of wings in the air, and a loud thump as something heavy hit the ground.

I needed to go to the bathroom so bad that I almost did. But I couldn't, because the biggest wild turkey gobbler in the world, I thought, entered the far edge of the pin oak flat.

The gobbler would pretend to peck around some, and then he would let out an earsplitting gobble, then he would strut. When he displayed (spread) his feathers, they made a loud scraping noise, as every feather scraped against another feather. It sent chills up my spine.

The range was right, plenty close, and the Doctor was ready. He had his shotgun propped up on his knee, and pointed in the general direction of the big gobbler. There would be no need for the fancy, store-bought turkey call hanging around the Doctor's neck.

But the Doctor didn't shoot. I was in a panic. I'd never heard of not shooting before.

The big turkey cocked his blue head to the side and listened to another turkey gobble in the near distance. Then he slicked his feathers down in one scraping motion, and headed off towards the other gobbler in that funny turkey trot.

We sat there for a few minutes longer, and then the Doctor said, "Lets go back." He put his hand on my shoulder and we walked back to the camp.

When we got to the camp, the Doctor checked his shotgun and then put it back into the leather case. His gun had not been loaded.

I sat in one of the Adirondack chairs by the ashes of our campfire while the Doctor made coffee with the remainder of a month's supply of coffee grounds. We quietly drank our coffee and listened to the occasional gobble of a turkey way off in the pin oak flats. We could hear the steady snoring of the driver coming from the cabin.

Finally the Doctor said, "This is the best hunt I've ever been on."

"Me, too," I said.

After a while the Doctor woke the driver and we all straightened things up in the cabin, and made sure the fire was safe out. Then the driver loaded our things into the turtle hull of the car and we headed for home.

When we got to my front yard, I got out of the car, and the driver got out, opened the turtle hull and handed me my bag.

I was walking toward the house when the driver said, "Wait a minute."

Then he handed me the hand tooled leather gun case, and said, "The Doc wants you to have this."

I took the gun case and stood there with my mouth open, in shock, while the driver got back into the car and they drove off, and out of sight.

That was the last time that we ever saw the Doctor.

Long years afterward, when I was grown, I tried to find out more about the Doctor, but all those who had known him and who he was, were gone.

The beautiful, gold inlaid shotgun occupies the place of honor in my gun cabinet. It's worth more than all of my other guns put together. I would never sell it; it means so much to me.

But I've never shot that beautiful shotgun. There's something about one barrel on top of the other barrel on a shotgun that just never seems right to me.

Chapter Twenty-Two
Neanderthal

Many thousands of years before God made Adam, He made a primitive form of man called Neanderthal man.

Archaeologists first found remains of this primitive form of man in the Neander Valley in Germany, thus the name Neanderthal [Neander Valley]. The h in thal is silent.

Neanderthals were robustly built with sharply sloping foreheads, distinct bony brow ridges, heavy bone structure, heavy muscular arms, and short stout legs. Examination of Neanderthal voice box areas indicates that they probably did not have a spoken language as modern man has.

Most scientists agree that when modern man appeared in the last great ice age, Neanderthal man and modern man coexisted but never together. Neanderthal man lived mostly in natural caves, and was well adapted to ice age living. As the last great ice age gradually ended, modern man became more numerous, and Neanderthal man became less numerous.

Most scientists believe that Neanderthal man died out and became extinct. However, at least one scientist believes that some Neanderthal people were assimilated into the modern man population.

In the summertime, Grandpa would let us ride into town on his old horse to get a snow cone and cool off. As I look back on it, I can see that the net result of riding seven miles into town to get a snow cone was counterproductive as to cooling off. I know it was counterproductive to Grandpa's old horse with three kids on his back.

We always took the old shortcut road beside the railroad through Shanty Town to the snow cone stand in town. Grandpa told us to never stop or get off of the horse in Shanty Town. And he told us to never get near the no-necks that lived in the big old run down house on the outskirts of Shanty Town.

We had heard about the no-necks from other kids at school. The daddy no-neck had a steeply sloping forehead and heavy brow ridges. And he had massive forearms and short stout legs. He had absolutely no neck. When he looked around, he had to turn his whole body because his head didn't swivel like ours do.

Mr. No-neck didn't work anywhere. People said that he was uneducated and didn't speak English.

All eight or ten of the no-neck kids went to school for a while but could not seem to achieve past the first grade. They all looked exactly like the father no-neck except for one who took after the mother. The one who took after the mother had at least three necks or chins, just like the mother had, and at least two bellies. One above the waist and one below. The one who looked like the mother did the talking for all of them, and he was bad mean.

Grandpa said for us to stay away from all of the no-necks, especially the girl ones. But I couldn't tell which ones were the girls and which ones were the boys. My best friend said that the boy no-necks had webbed feet, but you couldn't tell which ones had webbed feet because of the hair.

The no-necks didn't have electricity in the big old house that they stayed in. That wasn't unusual in those days. They gathered close around a fire after dark every night and kept the fire going until the sun came up in the morning. One night the fire burned down through the floor of the old house and liked to have burned the house down. The Volunteer fire crew had to come put it out. After that the no-necks stayed in the old barn behind the house. It was cooler in the barn, and they could control their animals better in the barn.

The firemen who put out the fire in the old house said that the inside walls were covered with drawings of stick men with no necks, and drawings of several kinds of local animals. And there were quite a few animal hides stretched and drying in various rooms.

Everybody used to dump surplus pets in Shanty Town, and it was a bad problem until the no-necks moved into town, then the surplus animal problem kind of went away. In fact, there were no loose animals within several blocks of the no-neck house in any direction.

One day the no-necks were just gone. I guess they assimilated into the population somewhere else.

Grandpa said, "Good riddance."

I said, "Grandpa! You always taught us not to be prejudiced against other races."

Grandpa said, "The no-necks weren't another race. They were another species."

Chapter Twenty-Three

Precious

I was playing in our back yard and when I saw the dust welling up out on the main dirt road. I knew it was some kind of trouble.

Sure enough, one of my best friend's brothers came riding up into our yard as fast as he could on his pony, and yelled that they needed Grandpa and Grandma as fast as possible, that his little baby sister had gone into the spring-house and fell in the water and was drowned.

Grandpa heard the commotion and came out on the porch. Grandpa said, "Did you call the doctor?"

My best friend's brother said, "No, it's too late! Precious is dead."

The little toddler's name was Precious. Her mom and dad had named her that because she came along so late in their lives, way after they thought that they were too old to have another child.

Seemed like people always called on Grandpa and Grandma when there was trouble in our neck of the woods. Grandpa was good at solving all kinds of problems and Grandma was sort of a midwife and a plant doctor. Grandma had delivered Precious and always said that she was the prettiest baby that she had ever delivered.

Grandpa and Grandma jumped in their old truck and I jumped in the back and away we went. Grandma always drove and usually she went slowly. But this time she went so fast it scared me sitting in the back.

It was only a couple of miles to the neighbors and when we got there they had Precious lying on the grass outside of the springhouse. She looked bad, sort of a mottled blue-gray color. She had been in that ice-cold spring water for a long time and she wasn't breathing and her heart wasn't beating.

I looked one time and then didn't want to look any more. It was so sad but I couldn't help watching.

My best friend was there and he was in shock or something, and so were his parents.

Grandpa and Grandma jumped out of the truck and Grandpa looked into the baby's little mouth and then he blew a little puff of breath into her mouth. Grandma started rubbing the little baby all over and mashing her chest a little, and Grandpa kept blowing little puffs of air into her tiny mouth and nose. Every once in a while they would tip the baby up on her side and sometimes a little water would run out of her mouth.

Grandpa and Grandma just kept doing the same thing over and over. They wouldn't stop.

People started arriving and it started getting to nighttime and getting colder. Some of the men built a big bonfire and it lit up the whole back yard, and you could see Grandpa breathing into the little baby, and Grandma massaging it all over and mashing its little chest.

Grandpa had bad knees and I knew it must have been killing him to kneel on that hard ground for so long. In between breaths I could see Grandpa's lips moving. I knew he was praying. I got close enough to hear him one time. Grandpa never would say ugly words or let us say ugly things or say the word hate, but I think I heard him say, "I hate you, Devil." But most of what I heard him saying was praying, and Grandma was praying too.

It got to be way up in the night and I guess I fell asleep on the truck seat, but some kind of commotion woke me up. Grandpa wasn't breathing into the little baby any more. He was still on his knees, but his face was pointed towards the sky and his hands were raised as high as he could raise them.

I looked at Grandma and she was holding Precious up to her chest and Precious' little eyes were open and she was making a little baby crying sound.

Grandma handed Precious to her mother and the biggest party

I've ever seen broke out.

The newspapers all said that Grandpa and Grandma brought the baby back to life. But Grandpa said that God brought the baby back to life. That all he and Grandma did was pray and do C.P.R. [Cardio Pulmonary Resuscitation].

Precious grew up to be a fine Christian evangelist. She travels all over preaching and bringing God's spiritual and physical healing to people. And when Precious describes the glorious wonders of Heaven, she's not talking from imagination, she's talking from memory.

Chapter Twenty-Four
The Battle

Grandpa had a perfect record. He never lost a battle. But one time he came very close. It was a battle with a dog.

Grandpa was never without at least one beagle from the time he got his first one as a kid, until he passed away. Grandpa loved to run rabbits with his beagles, and he was very proud of them. For the most part, they were good clean rabbit beagles that didn't run trash.

I was Grandpa's rabbit hunting partner and had the privilege of helping him tend the beagles, like washing out the pens, and giving shots and worm pills. And Grandpa treated his beagles real good. He said that they would run their hearts out for us, and they did.

One year Grandpa's younger brother, my great uncle, gave Grandpa his beagle yard dog, because Great Uncle was moving to a place where they didn't allow dogs.

It was a beautiful male beagle named Nelson, Nellie for short. Nellie looked just like the picture you would see if you looked up beagle in the encyclopedia.

In fact, Nellie might have been registered. If so, he was the only dog that Grandpa ever had that was registered. Because registration papers don't run rabbits, Grandpa always said.

And Grandpa never bought a dog either. He would raise his own, or somebody would give Grandpa a pup in return for beagle stud service. Grandpa never required a pup in payment for stud service, but occasionally he would accept one if he needed a pup at the time.

The first time that we took Nellie out to run, he got on a deer. We ran him down and carried him a ways off of the deer scent. I remember that when you carried Nellie, his legs would move like he was running. He looked just like a mechanical dog.

When we set Nellie back down on the ground, he immediately ran back to the deer trail. So we caught him again, and Grandpa gave him a good spanking with his belt. Then we let him go again, and he immediately fell in on the deer trail again, harder than ever.

When we got home, Grandpa ordered a big bottle of deer break scent from the hunting dog supply catalog. When the break scent came in, we rubbed it on Nellie's nose and mouth, and did it ever stink! We rubbed it on Nellie every day until that big bottle was used up.

It just about broke me from ever wanting to go deer hunting again. But when we took Nellie out to the woods again, he got on a hot deer trail, and stayed gone all night.

Deer season opened and Grandpa got a fresh deer skin and wound it all around Nellie's collar and made him wear it until he finally got it all chewed off.

We took Nellie to the woods and he hit a deer trail and took it out of hearing. He was getting to where he would watch ahead with one eye and watch for Grandpa and me with the other eye. And he was starting to get hard to catch.

But we finally got him back. Then Grandpa took a fresh deer skin and cut four leg holes in it, and put Nellie in the skin with his legs through the holes, and hoisted him up on a long rope hanging from a tree limb. Then we swung Nellie round and round until we were so dizzy that we couldn't spin him any more.

The next day we took Nellie to the woods again. Nellie was barely clear of the truck tailgate when he hit a deer trail and headed south.

Seven days later, Grandpa got a call from a farmer down on the parish line. He said that he had a dog with Grandpa's name and phone number on the collar, shut up in his woodshed.

We went down to the old farmer's house and he came out to meet us in the front yard. The farmer said that every day for six days a beagle had come across his back pasture headed south into the other parish behind a deer, and every afternoon the same beagle would come back across the pasture headed north running deer.

The farmer said that on the seventh day the beagle came up to his house looking for food, he guessed, so he put him in the wood shed and called Grandpa from his name and number on the collar.

The farmer said that Nellie was all heart.

I picked Nellie up and put him in the truck. He weighed about a third of his normal weight. He looked like a skeleton with rawhide stretched over it, and he sure was glad to see Grandpa and me.

We put him in the dog box and started home. After a while I said, "Grandpa, if Nellie can't stop doing wrong, we're going to have to get rid of him."

After a long while Grandpa said, "Son, it's not Nellie that's doing wrong. It's us."

"How's that Grandpa?" I asked.

Grandpa said, "Nellie's not a rabbit dog, he's a deer dog."

Chapter Twenty-Five
Tracks

Grandpa was a good hunter, but he didn't brag about it.

Three miles down the road from Grandpa lived a family of hunters that didn't brag about it either. They didn't have to brag. Their hunting exploits were legendary.

The father worked in the mill and raised cows on their small farm. There were two adult sons who lived in their own homes on the old family farm. One of the sons was a forester and the other was a wildlife biologist.

It was a mystery to most people how this family of hunters could kill deer, or turkeys, or ducks, or whatever was in season, even when other hunters couldn't kill a thing.

It wasn't a mystery to me. I knew how they did it. I just didn't know how they found the time, because they all three had full time jobs and families to look after.

They did it by scouting and knowing what the animals were doing, and where and when they were doing it. All three of the men were good Christians and they went to our church, and they saw Grandpa at Church service on Wednesday nights, and on Sunday, and on other special occasions, like revivals and such.

Grandpa liked to have his deer stand where nobody else hunted. He hid his stand and didn't tell anyone, other than family, where it was.

But after church, when Grandpa and Grandma were visiting with other church members, Mr. Hunter would say, "If you move your stand a hundred yards further north you would get a nice ten point buck." Or, "If you hunted on the other side of the old slough, you would get a gobbler with a thirteen-inch beard."

Mr. Hunter always told Grandpa some intimate detail of Grandpa's hunting territory, and Grandpa checked it out and Mr. Hunter was always right.

One time Grandpa got upset and moved his stand a mile in the wrong direction. And at church the next day Mr. Hunter said, "You put your stand in a good place for does and fawns, but if you would have gone fifty yards further, you'd be on a big eight point."

Grandpa said that Mr. Hunter knew the first name of every animal in the Parish.

The hallway in Mr. Hunter's house was lined with mounted trophy deer heads and every mounted head had other big deer antlers hanging on them, and piled up on top of them.

There was a place in the piney woods, a couple of miles from Mr. Hunter's farm where nobody hunted because it was devoid of any kind of game animal. It was a big tract of barren pineland, with a timber company dirt road through the middle.

Every year the timber company graded the old dirt road and Grandpa walked the road looking for Indian arrowheads, and deer or turkey tracks. He found a few arrowheads there, but he never found any deer or turkey tracks.

One spring, about a month before turkey season, the timber company graded the road, and Grandpa hatched a plan to test Mr. Hunter.

Grandpa took an old pair of thick-soled boots into his workshop, and carved twelve-inch long turkey tracks on the bottom. He made one track point forward, and one track point rearward, so that when he walked it would look like a huge turkey had walked up the road and back, with a stride of over five feet.

Grandpa did a good job carving the tracks into the boot soles, and he copied a real turkey foot. In the soft dirt of the fresh graded road, the tracks looked real.

That evening at Wednesday night service, Mr. Hunter told Grandpa that he had found the biggest turkey tracks that he had ever seen. He didn't say where, but his truck was seen parked on the old dirt road in the barren pines on several occasions.

On the first Sunday after turkey season opened, Mr. Hunter told Grandpa, "I didn't get the big turkey that I was after, but I got a nice gobbler with a nineteen inch beard, and it weighed twenty-eight pounds near the old dirt road through the barren pines. Mr. Hunter said, "I guess the big turkey that I was after was just passing through looking for arrowheads."

Chapter Twenty-Six
The Fishing Camp

I've always been shy, or you might say scared, of girls. Up through high school, I don't guess I ever had a real date with a girl. I was always too shy to ask a girl out. And I figure it kept me out of a lot of trouble.

Oh, I knew girls could work their way around a boy's shyness if they wanted to. But I was never considered handsome or exciting, so they didn't bother with me. I've had good friends who were girls, but never a girlfriend.

One day, just after I graduated from high school, Grandpa asked me if I would accompany him on an all day trip.

I said, "Sure."

Grandpa and I left at daylight the next morning in his old truck, prepared to be gone all day. Grandpa started driving south. After about an hour, Grandpa asked me to drive. Whenever he went anywhere in the truck with Grandma, she drove, and since she wasn't with us, he let me drive.

Grandpa told me which roads to take and we continued to head south. By midmorning we were out of the low hills of our part of Louisiana, and into flat country. We drove through miles and miles of cotton, corn, and swamp. We stopped for gas at a little town where the first language was French.

By noon we had eaten up all of the sandwiches that grandma had sent for our lunch, but Grandpa wouldn't stop for more lunch. He was determined to get to our destination.

By mid-afternoon we were in a country of water and marsh grass. The roads were built up on top of levees with water on both sides. We passed small cemeteries where the graves were on top of the ground in tombs so that the caskets wouldn't be below the water table.

Houses were perched on small house sites constructed on the shoulder of the road. Their back yards were wharves in the canal, and many had beautiful old-fashioned shrimp boats and fishing boats that looked like sailing boats tied up to the wharves.

We drove until the blacktop ended and an oyster shell road continued. At the end of the oyster shell road, we came to a fishing camp. It was an unpainted building, with water on three sides, a small oyster shell parking lot, a few skiffs for rent, a pier on the back, and a big tank with a sign that said, "Live Shrimp".

The lawn of the fishing camp was a small patch of lawn grass with a homemade picnic table sitting in the shade of a hackberry tree. It was the only tree that we had seen in the last couple of miles.

Sitting at the picnic table was an old gray-haired man and an old gray-haired woman.

We parked the truck and got out, and when the old man and woman recognized Grandpa, they hugged and kissed him, and there were tears of joy in three sets of old eyes.

Grandpa introduced me, and the old man and woman were so excited. They talked with a strong accent, and they talked both at the same time, about three different things at once, and they asked questions in rapid fire, but never gave us a chance to answer.

Finally Grandpa got a word in edgewise, and he asked where their son J.R. was, and where their grandchild C.R. was. J.R. didn't stand for anything; it was their son's name.

The old folks said that J.R. and C.R. were out in the boat, and that they would be back soon. But time doesn't mean the same thing to those people as it does to us, we found out.

They showed us around their house. The first thing that you notice about somebody else's house is how it smells. And their house smelled very different. It smelled very good, spicy, salty, and clean.

There were all manner of things that were unusual to me hanging on the walls. Like fishnets, deep-sea floats, driftwood, and old boat fittings, which I did not recognize.

After the tour, we relocated back outside to the picnic table under the hackberry tree. The old grandma fixed us big glasses of ice-cold lemonade, and we listened to the old man and woman talk about three things at once.

By late afternoon, I was starting to wonder how long "soon" meant, when the old grandpa, who couldn't see up close to find his own glasses, spotted a speck on the water at the horizon. And he said, "Here comes J.R."

An hour later the speck had grown into a beautiful sculptured fishing boat that looked like a sleek sailboat without a mast.

Another half an hour and that boat was tied up to the pier at the fishing camp, and J.R. was striding across the small yard to greet Grandpa. And C.R. was striding beside him, and she wasn't a child.

C.R. was a full-grown eighteen-year-old girl with coal black eyes, long straight dark brown hair, and a slender, but muscular figure. She was brown as a nut from working in the sun on the fishing boat. J.R. introduced C.R. to me as CoRenna.

I'm not sure what happened next, but CoRenna and I were all of a sudden sitting on opposite sides of the picnic table, with huge glasses of lemonade, and Grandpa, J.R., and J.R.'s parents were gone somewhere. Gone into the fishing camp, I guess.

I had not said a word yet, but that didn't matter. CoRenna was talking about three different things at once, and asking rapid-fire questions that I couldn't answer because I was smitten from the top of my head to my toenails. I was struck speechless.

CoRenna was looking deep into my eyes and she saw the problem, so she paused for a second, which gave me time to blurt out, "Will you marry me and move to north Louisiana?"

CoRenna said, "Yes."

It was the best decision that either of us has ever made.

When we got home late that night, actually early the next morning, and told Mom about everything, she said, "You didn't take very long to think this over."

I said, "I didn't need to. Grandpa and the Good Lord had planned this out a long time ago."

Chapter Twenty-Seven

Lost

Grandpa never got lost. I asked him one time if he had ever been lost?

He said, "No." He told me that he always carried a compass when he went into the woods.

I don't know if Grandpa got the quote right, or even the person quoted right, but he told me that somebody once asked the famous woodsman, Daniel Boone, if he had ever been lost?

Mr. Boone replied, "No, but I've been confused several times."

Grandpa said that being lost was a state-of-mind, not a place-of-location.

Several years ago, when my little niece was two and a half or three years old, we were in a church service in our church. My little niece always sat on Grandma's lap through the church service, and often went to sleep with her head on Grandma's shoulder.

In this particular service, when we stood up to sing, my niece spotted Nanny, my sister, across the aisle and a couple of pews back, and she wouldn't have anything else except to go to Nanny. And Grandma was always a soft touch where the little ones were concerned, so she took my niece across the aisle and handed her to Nanny.

That lasted for the usual attention span of a two-year-old, and then my niece demanded to go back to Grandma. So Nanny put her on the floor and pointed her back to Grandma.

I was watching when the little one made it to the aisle and turned to find the pew that Grandma was in.

But the little one was too short to see over the pews of seated people, and she couldn't see Grandma, and she didn't know which way to go.

My little niece has always been shy and scary, and I saw the realization of being lost come over her face. In complete terror, she hollered out, "Meemaw!" And Grandma stood up and stretched her arms out to the little one, who saw her above the people and ran to the safety of her arms. There was much kissing and hugging, and the little one settled down to a contented nap on Grandma's lap.

My niece matured into a fine adult woman, completed nursing school, and started a career in a prestigious hospital in the city.

As my niece got more into the city-life culture, she drifted further away from our church standards. She cut her hair short and changed its color, and she wore more and more makeup. She slowly lost sight of her Christian destination. She never was bad, but she became lost. She came to believe that her life was meaningless and hopeless.

In the middle of the night one night she considered ending her life. But instead she went down on her knees and in desperation cried out, "Jesus!" And He stood up and stretched His arms out to her and she came back to Him. There was much repentative crying, and she was no longer lost. He had been there all the time. She just couldn't see Him over all the things that had gotten in the way.

Most birds and animals have a guidance system that people call instinct, but it is probably a physical thing controlled by the magnetic field of the earth, like a compass needle is controlled.

People said that Grandpa had that instinct, but I think that Grandpa was just very familiar with most of the woods for miles around. I know for a fact that when Grandpa went into strange woods, he always carried and used a compass.

And Grandpa had a strong instinct as to the direction of his Christian goal, too. And I know for a fact that he kept on course by keeping and using his Christian compass, the Holy Bible.

Chapter Twenty-Eight
Education

I went to elementary school in a one-room schoolhouse, high school in town, and to college at the State University, but I got my education at Grandpa's knee.

Grandpa could explain things so that I could understand. I think teachers could do that if they knew how and had time. But then again, some things are better learned at home or at church.

When I was in the first grade, some big boys told me that I shouldn't be friends with Junior because his skin was a different color from mine. I asked Grandpa about it.

Grandpa said, "Son, you've been friends with Junior all of your life. It's your responsibility to judge who is fit to be your friend based on things like loyalty, truthfulness, and other things of good character. It doesn't have anything to do with skin color."

When I was in the second grade, a mean girl started picking on me all the time and she said that she was going to beat me up. The boys teased me about it, and said that if I wasn't a sissy, I would fight her and make her stop persecuting me. I asked Grandpa about it.

Grandpa said, "Son, we've always taught you not to hit anybody smaller or weaker than yourself, and don't ever hit a girl. The only kind of a boy that would hit someone or something weaker than himself, or a girl, is a coward and a bully."

I said, "But Grandpa, this girl is a lot bigger and stronger than I am."

Grandpa said, "In that case, son, you are impaled on the horns of a dilemma." Grandpa continued, "A dilemma is a problem that has two answers, but both of them are bad, like the two horns of a bull."

I said, "What are the two answers here, Grandpa?"

Grandpa said, "One answer is to fight back and hit this girl. But then you would forever be known as a coward and a bully and a girl hitter."

I said, "What's the other answer, Grandpa?"

Grandpa said, "Son, do you know what the fetal position is?"

When I was in the third grade we stopped having our morning prayer in school. I asked Grandpa, "The teacher said we couldn't pray in school any more. That it is against the law. Is that right?"

Grandpa said, "No, son. That's not right. You can pray all you want in school. It's against the law for the teacher in a government school to teach children how to pray."

I asked, "Why's that, Grandpa?"

Grandpa said, "Because a lot of the teachers are not qualified to teach you how to pray the way your parents and your pastor want you to pray. Some of the teachers are not Christians. Some are even Devil worshipers, they have a teachers' union, and they will claim religious discrimination if they are fired. But you can pray all you want in school, as long as you don't disrupt class.

I know your teacher. She is a good Christian. But other schools aren't so lucky. Prayer should be taught in the home and in the church, not in government schools."

In the fourth grade, a boy whom I thought was my friend, lied on purpose, and got me in trouble with the teacher.

I explained it to Grandpa and he said, "Son, it's your responsibility to judge whether someone is worthy of your friendship. A liar is not worthy of being your friend. Don't waste your time listening to what a liar says. What liars say is worthless. The Bible directly commands people not to lie, and those that do lie are lost."

When I was in the sixth grade some big boys tried to get me to smoke a cigarette. I knew better than to do it, but my best friend said that he would try anything once.

I asked Grandpa, "Is my friend right by trying anything once?"

Grandpa said, "Son, I hope your friend isn't stupid enough to try jumping out of an airplane without a parachute just once."

In the seventh grade, the big boys would bring beer to the Friday night dances and drink it behind the adults' backs. They tried to get me to drink some. They said that everybody was doing it.

I didn't drink any, but I told Grandpa that they said that everybody was doing it.

Grandpa said, " Son, if everybody jumped off of a cliff, would you jump off, too?"

I said, "Grandpa, we don't have any cliffs around here."

Chapter Twenty-Nine
The Gift

We used to play cork ball after school when we were kids. The pitcher would pitch a cork ball and the batter would try to hit it with a broom handle. And we had bases and fowl lines like in a baseball game.

But you didn't need bases when my first cousin was pitching, because nobody could hit his pitch.

In high school, cousin pitched for the school baseball team, and nobody could hit his pitch there either.

Cousin didn't go to college because a big league team drafted him straight out of high school. Cousin was Rookie-of-the-Year his first year in the big league, and almost Player-of-the-Year.

The other players said that cousin chunked the ball so hard that you could barely see it, much less hit it. So from then on everybody called my cousin, Chunk.

Chunk became the most famous person in north Louisiana. Probably the most famous person in all of Louisiana.

Most of the reporters didn't like Chunk, because he wouldn't do interviews. See, Chunk inherited a disability sometimes passed down in our family, called Genetic Shyness. It didn't bother Chunk on the ballfield because he focused on the ballgame and shut everything else out entirely. But off of the ballfield he avoided most contact with strangers, if he could. He was better around family, but he couldn't put two words together in a sentence to a stranger. He even avoided talking on the phone.

During the off-season, Chunk signed a big contract for a lot of money. And on his first pitch of his second season, Chunk felt something pop in his throwing arm elbow, and his baseball career was over. He had an operation and could use his arm pretty well, but he could never play baseball again. A big insurance policy paid off, and Chunk invested the money and was fixed financially.

To have something productive to keep him busy, Chunk took a job with a timber company, marking timber. Chunk loved to be out in the woods and away from strangers.

Chunk usually didn't pick up the phone when it rang, but he had a telephone answering machine, and he'd listen to the calls most of the time. Usually it was somebody who wanted him to donate some money to some cause, or speak at a mall opening or something like that, and Chunk never returned the calls.

One Friday night a call came in, and it was from the principal of the high school in a small town nearby. The caller said, "I'm sorry to bother you. I know you don't do interviews or make public appearances, but I can't think of anywhere else to turn. We've tried everything we know, but our school kids keep going in the wrong direction. Smoking, drinking, drugs, sex, and fighting are going up, and grades are going down ever since the courts banned prayer in our school.

If you could come to our assembly Monday morning, and speak to the kids for fifteen minutes, you might inspire at least one of them to do better.

I'll hang up now. Thank you."

Before the principal could hang up, Chunk picked up his phone and said, "I'll be there."

Chunk didn't sleep a minute Friday, Saturday, or Sunday nights. All he did was toss and turn and downrate himself for accepting the invitation to talk to the kids on Monday.

But he said he'd do it, so he'd do it. And on Monday morning, Chunk showed up at the high school at assembly time. The principal led him to the center of the stage in the auditorium, pointed him to the lectern, and introduced him to the noisy crowd of kids.

The kids were throwing spitballs, hollering, and carrying on in general. Some were sitting on the backs of their seats, and some were slouched down like they were in reclining chairs.

Chunk would have given anything to be somewhere else. He would have tried to hide behind the lectern, but he was a big, tall man, and the lectern only came up to his waist.

Chunk tried to say something, but he could only stammer. The kids laughed at him and did cat calls, but Chunk tried again. But again, he could only stammer. The kids saw his head turn down in shame, they thought. But they could see his lips moving and they saw tears pouring out of his eyes. And they began to quieten down because unbeknownst to Chunk, the microphone was picking up his whispers, and the kids were listening.

Chunk was praying. And he prayed for the kids, and for their teachers, and for their school, and for their parents.

Finally Chunk looked up and saw that the kids were sitting on the edge of their seats listening, and you could hear a pin drop in that auditorium. The only sound was a few of the girls crying softly.

Chunk began to speak, and he had the most beautiful, soft voice, with a beautiful southern country accent. And he began to tell the kids all the things that Grandpa had taught him as he was growing up, and how those teachings had influenced his life, and many other peoples' lives.

The bell rung, but Chunk didn't stop talking, and not a single person left the auditorium, and for over two hours, nobody spoke a word except Chunk. And Chunk never said a word about baseball.

Chunk ended by saying that the kids were the nicest bunch of young men and women that he had ever seen. And every person in that auditorium crowded across the stage, and every one of them shook Chunk's hand and thanked him for coming.

In that high school, grades went up, and smoking, drinking, drugs, and violence went way down.

The word spread like wildfire, and Chunk's answering machine couldn't keep up with the flood of calls asking him to speak at schools and churches and such, all across the state. And Chunk did speak at as many of them as he could, sometimes two on the same night.

And it never was any easier for Chunk to speak than it was the first time. He couldn't put two words together until he had prayed long and deep.

The baseball man told Grandpa that he didn't understand why God would give a man such a gift as he gave Chunk, and then take it away with an injury.

Grandpa said, "God didn't take away Chunk's gift. He took baseball away because it was blocking the way of Chunk's true gift."

Chapter Thirty
The Accident

Every once in a while Grandpa had to go into town to the feed store. Grandma would drive the truck because Grandpa's eyesight wasn't what it used to be.

After they went to the feed store, they would go to the big chain store supermarket, so that they could pick up a few necessities.

While in the supermarket one day, Grandpa's hip gave away, and he fell, and was taken to the hospital. Grandpa had surgery on his hip, and was recovering fine, and was scheduled to go home from the hospital in about a week.

Grandpa had a visitor who came to the hospital to see him right after the accident. The visitor was a well-dressed young woman, very personable, and very attractive. When the young lady asked to speak to Grandpa, Grandma stayed in the hospital room for two reasons:

The first reason was that Grandpa had a policy of never being alone with any woman except Grandma.

The second reason was that Grandma had a policy of never leaving Grandpa alone with any woman except herself.

The young lady introduced herself as a representative of the company that owned the supermarket chain, which owned the supermarket that Grandpa had broken his hip in.

The young lady said that her company wanted to pay Grandpa's hospital bill and his doctor's bill, and to pay him for his pain and suffering.

Grandpa told the lady that it wasn't the supermarket's fault that his hip had broken, and that his insurance and Medicare would pay the hospital and doctor's bill. And that Grandma took care of all of his pain and suffering.

The young lady talked a while longer, but seeing that she wasn't making any progress with Grandpa, she politely excused herself and left.

The next day a sharply dressed man, in a tailored three-piece suit and carrying a leather briefcase, arrived at Grandpa's hospital room.

Grandma said that he looked like a Philadelphia Lawyer.

The man told Grandpa that he worked for the company that owned the supermarket chain that owned the supermarket where Grandpa had broken his hip. The man told Grandpa that his company had never failed to settle accident claims connected with their supermarkets and that he was authorized to make Grandpa an offer that was guaranteed to satisfy him.

Grandpa tried to explain to the man that it wasn't the supermarket's fault that he had broken his hip, but he couldn't break through. The man had his mind made up.

The man took a check out of his briefcase and laid it face down, on the night table beside Grandpa's hospital bed. The man said, "I'm leaving this check to cover your hospital and doctors' expenses, and your pain and suffering. I know that you will find that it is a very generous payment."

Grandpa said, "I give up."

The man left, and Grandpa took the ballpoint pen that was lying on the night table, and without looking at the front of the check, he endorsed the check, and wrote under his endorsement: Pay to the order of the Pentecostal Church.

Then he folded the check and handed it to Grandma, and asked her to put it in the collection plate at church on Sunday, which she did.

Grandpa got out of the hospital in a week or so and recovered nicely.

Our church blacktopped the parking lot, and added a wing of Sunday school rooms to the church building. And they didn't have to borrow money to do it.

Grandpa eventually got over losing the argument to the man.

You know Grandpa. He had a way of winning, even when he lost.

Chapter Thirty-One
The Sin

My Dad's brothers and sisters all had big families, my Dad had two sons and two daughters.

I was about thirty years old when Dad retired. I ran a little business of my own. It usually paid the expenses and was starting to show a profit now and then.

Grandpa had been retired for nearly twenty years when Dad retired. Dad had worked for a huge company for thirty-five years, and he was highly respected in the company and he moved up in management and drew a nice paycheck.

Dad's company gave him a retirement banquet in their conference hall, and all the company big shots came. The tables were arranged in a big tee, with the dignitaries seated across the top of the tee, and the rank and file seated on both sides of the long leg of the tee.

Dad was seated in the middle, and the company President, and the Chief Executive Officer and several Vice Presidents were on both sides. The company officers were dressed immaculately in expensive foreign-made suits and Italian shoes.

Dad was allowed to bring two guests, so he brought Grandpa and me, and we sort of kept out of the way, down on the end. I wore my best suit, which cost less than a hundred dollars at the time. Grandpa wore casual clothes, but he did put on an old black suit jacket over his sport shirt.

Waiters served a fancy meal, and Dad cut the big fancy cake. When we were nearly through eating, the Vice-president in charge of Dad's division came up to the lectern and made a big speech about how valuable an employee Dad had been, and how much the company was going to miss him.

Then the Personnel Director came up to the lectern and presented Dad with a beautiful, engraved Browning Citori Shotgun. And he asked Dad to say a few words.

Dad stood at the lectern and said, "I've enjoyed working for this company, and as companies go, it is the best. And the people who work here are the best, and they will always be in my memories.

Dad Continued, "One thing I want to do is to recognize the two men who have taught me so much over these years. These are the two men in the world that I would most like to be like, and they mean the world to me."

The CEO and the Company President exchanged glances. They knew Dad was talking about them. The Vice President of Dad's division had a smug look on his face. He knew Dad was talking about him.

Dad left the lectern and walked toward the Company President, and the CEO, and the Vice President, and they pushed their chairs back a little so that they could rise.

But Dad walked past them and stopped behind Grandpa and me. Then he pulled us to our feet and hugged us, and there were tears in his eyes when he said, "This is my father and my son."

And that's when I committed the sin of pridefullness. And I can't help it.

Chapter Thirty-Two

Luck

The year started off bad for Grandpa and Grandma.

Grandma had her checkup and the doctor found cancer. She had surgery, chemotherapy, and radiation, and God cured her of the cancer. Her checkups have all been good since. Thank God.

While Grandma was in the hospital for her surgery, the hot water heater at Grandpa and Grandma's house started leaking and ruined quite a good bit of the flooring.

Grandpa got a new water heater, and while he was installing it, and replacing the floor, he found termites. The termites were in the foundation of the house, in the floor, and some in the walls.

Grandpa poisoned the termites and saved most of the house, but his yard dog and a couple of hogs that stayed under the house died. Grandpa said that he wanted to be sure that he got all of the termites. I think he did.

Summer came and we had no rain. Grandpa's garden didn't make anything. Grandma didn't have any vegetables to can and she and Grandpa used up all of the home canned food in the pantry.

Finally Grandma went into town and bought food at the grocery. Grandpa almost starved before he would eat the bought food. Grandma said that he was spoiled.

The no rain situation became a drought. Grandpa's artesian well went dry for the first time ever. Grandpa had a new deep well drilled and it had a good flow of water. But Grandpa said that it didn't taste as good as the artesian well water. He was right about that.

Grandpa took his truck to my uncle for a tune-up. But when my uncle got into it, he found that the block was broken and Grandpa needed another motor.

The piney woods got so dry that wild fires were breaking out every day. Grandpa and my Dad were gone a lot, helping backfire away from the neighbors' houses and barns.

One day while Grandpa was gone, his best rabbit dog got out. The hardheaded boy dog was an escape artist. He wanted to hunt all the time, whether it was rabbit season or not, and he could get out of most any pen.

Grandpa would usually let him run rabbits out back until he got tired and then put him back in the pen. This time, for some reason, the dog headed all the way out to the main highway, and that's where Dad and Grandpa found his flattened body.

The pond got so low that the catfish died from lack of oxygen. They were mostly pets. Grandpa and Grandma liked to feed them and watch them eat.

Our preacher took the opportunity to preach hard and long about the Tribulation. It was scary.

The doctor told Grandma to walk thirty minutes each day, and he told Grandpa that walking would be good for him, too. So Grandpa and Grandma walked thirty minutes every day.

I would wait for them on my porch, and when they got to my driveway I would join in and walk with them until we got back to my driveway. I enjoyed it very much, and looked forward to it each day.

One day I saw them coming along in the distance, holding hands like they always did, and swing their two hands way up. Grandpa was talking, and Grandma was laughing and giggling.

When I joined them, I asked Grandpa a question. Grandpa was a deep thinker, and was known to philosophize about things.

I asked him what all this bad luck meant. I figured that it would take him at least the rest of our walk to answer.

Grandpa looked at Grandma. Her eyes were bright and sparkling like a young girl's. Grandma gave Grandpa a big warm smile.

Grandpa turned back to me and said, "Son, all that don't mean a thing."

Chapter Thirty-Three
Three Generations

It was black dark when the three hunters left their truck in the predawn of the opening day of muzzle-loading season for deer. My uncle quietly led the way into the woods. Barely two hundred yards from the truck he stopped and whispered to the boy, "Here's your stand, son. We'll be back and get you here about ten o'clock. Good luck and be careful."

My uncle and Grandpa walked on. It was the first time my cousin had been left alone on a stand, and my uncle had mixed feelings of anxiety and pride. He knew the boy would follow all the safety rules, and that he would be quiet and ready if a deer did come by.

Grandpa remembered as he walked behind my uncle. He remembered when he walked ahead and led his son to stands that he had located. Now it was different Grandpa thought with pride. His strong son could name almost every plant or tree that he passed. He knew the name of the animals, insects, snakes, and birds that he would see. He knew the kinds of rock and how they were formed, and he knew the type of locations to look for Indian artifacts.

While not seeming to particularly notice anything, he missed nothing. He could read deer sign like a book. If asked about a deer track, he could casually comment on the size and sex of the deer, and where it was probably going, and why and when. Grandpa smiled to himself, thinking how much his grandson was like his son.

Two hundred yards farther into the woods my uncle and Grandpa reached the second stand location. No words were necessary and none were spoken. Just a pat on the back and a lip-shaped, "Good luck", and my uncle continued on alone while Grandpa stayed at the second stand.

My uncle fussed to himself a little as he reached his stand fifteen minutes later as the sky was already getting lighter.

A few minutes after daylight, my uncle heard the woof-boom of the boy's flintlock. He restrained his strong urge to go to the boy. He knew that one of the hardest things for a parent to do is to let a child grow up. He knew the deer was down. He had watched the boy practice with the long flintlock that Grandpa had made, and though the rifle was longer than the boy was tall, he could shoot it from a rest. And if he shot, he hit, because he didn't pull the trigger unless the sights were on the target. The boy had a lot of play in him, but when it came to shooting or hunting, he was as serious as a prayer.

About 9:30 a.m., my uncle got down from his stand and started back toward his father's stand. My uncle had seen a small buck, which he passed up to let it grow larger for some future year.

When my uncle walked up to his father's stand, Grandpa was standing there impatiently waiting. "Did you see any, Dad?" my uncle asked.

Grandpa answered, "I saw a nice buck but didn't get a shot." He didn't tell his son that he had not climbed up into the stand because he didn't think he could climb safely any longer. He also didn't tell him that the spectacular buck had stood in the small clearing close by for several minutes, but that every time he tried to aim his old flintlock, the sights were so blurred that he couldn't be sure of an accurate shot.

My uncle walked quickly now, pausing often to let Grandpa catch up so that they could arrive at the boy's stand together.

When they reached the opening, they saw the boy proudly standing by a big doe which he had already field dressed.

My uncle fought down the strong urge to grab up the boy and swing him round and round as he had so often done. Instead he reached out his hand, shook the boy's hand in a firm grip, and said one word: "Beautiful."

Grandpa in unrestrained emotion, bear-hugged the boy, and then danced a stiff-legged jig all around the small clearing.

"How'd it happen?" my uncle asked the boy.

The boy said, "Three does came up. I waited until I could pick the dominant doe, then I took her."

"How'd you feel about it?" my uncle asked.

"A little sad, a lot glad. I knew that removing her would help the younger deer and improve the habitat, just like you taught me."

"What'd you do after you shot?" my uncle asked.

The boy said, "I waited a few minutes, then I got down from the stand and followed the blood trail. I found her about twenty yards from the clearing."

"Then what?" my uncle asked.

"I said a little prayer," the boy said. "I thanked God for the beautiful doe, and I thanked God for giving my Dad the time to teach me right from wrong and what is important in this life. And I thanked God for giving my Grandpa the time to make me that beautiful flintlock rifle."

My uncle looked at Grandpa and saw the tears of happiness and pride in his old eyes, and knew that Grandpa could see the same in his.

This morning, father, son, and grandfather, all three, experienced the highest degree of success, not easily understood by non-hunters.

The good old days are now.

Chapter Thirty-Four

Grandma

As far as I know, Grandma only had two moods: smiling or laughing.

When the grandkids came over to Grandpa's and Grandma's, the first thing they would say to Grandpa was, "Where's Grandma?" if she was out of sight.

Grandma gave good hugs, and she always kept a glass bowl of gumdrops in her China cabinet.

When we got the word that Grandma had fallen out at a Ladies meeting, and had to be taken to the hospital, I went by and picked up Grandpa and we rushed to the hospital emergency room. Grandpa was silent and grimfaced all the way there.

Grandpa and Grandma had bonded and become one person over seventy years before. I truly believe that they had never knowingly spoken an unkind word to each other in that whole time.

In an age when women were usually expected to yield to the wishes of their husbands, Grandpa always acknowledged Grandma as an equal. Although Grandma did follow the *Bible* teaching, that the husband had the responsibility of making the final decision when a question arose. They both realized that neither one could be happy unless the other one was first happy. In other words, the true definition of love.

We got to the hospital before the others did, and the nurse at the emergency room door told us that we needed to go right in.

When we entered the room, I thought there had been a mistake and that we had gone into the wrong room. We were here to see Grandma, not the frail elderly woman lying pale on the hospital bed with such a lifeless expression on her face.

Grandpa went to the bedside and took the old woman's hand and whispered something in her ear, and for a minute she turned back into Grandma. Her eyes lit up and her smile came back as she looked at Grandpa and then she was gone.

The others started getting there by ones and twos, and pretty soon the hospital hall was crowded and there was a lot of crying going on.

Grandpa went to each one and hugged them, and told them that Grandma was already in the most beautiful and happiest place that anybody could ever be. And that she was no longer in the prison of that frail old body, and that she was in the presence of Jesus our Lord.

Then Grandpa asked me to take him home.

When we got to Grandpa's, I asked him the stupid question that people always ask at a time like this, "Are you going to be all right, Grandpa?"

It's never all right to lie, but at a time like this people will, just to make other people feel better. Grandpa said, "I'll be all right."

We started taking turns staying at Grandpa's every night, but we soon could tell that he needed somebody around full time, so he moved in with Mom and Dad. They lived next door, and he could still work in his workshop whenever he wanted, and Mom could keep an eye on him without trying to interfere with his freedom.

Grandpa usually worked in his workshop every day. He was building a flintlock rifle, and it takes a long time to build a flintlock when you do it right. And Grandpa always built them right.

Grandpa got frail and he had to use a magnifying visor to see his work, but he worked like he was obsessed with finishing that rifle. Usually Mom had to go to his workshop and talk him into stopping at night so that he could get some rest.

Then one day about noon, Grandpa completed the flintlock rifle and he and his old dog got in his old truck and went to the swamp. And he went to his favorite deer hunting place and sat down against his favorite tree and he passed away.

Everybody said that Grandpa waited until he finished that flintlock rifle to die. But that's not right. Grandpa died that day in the hospital when Grandma died.

Chapter Thirty-Five
The Decoy

The decoy was gone. It had been sitting in the same place on the fireplace mantel for nearly fifty years, but now it was gone.

Grandpa had made it and gave it to my Dad a long time ago. And Dad treasured it, and kept it in the most prominent place in the house, on the fireplace mantel. And Dad never had let us play with that decoy, or even hold it without close supervision.

Grandpa had made the decoy in the old-fashioned way, by hand, out of the swollen butt of a big cypress tree from the swamp out behind the house. The decoy was graceful and beautiful, and somehow you just liked to look at it. And Dad wouldn't have taken anything for it. But it was gone and Dad was upset.

Dad asked all of us where the decoy was, but we didn't know. So he went out in Grandpa's workshop where Grandpa was sitting in his rocking chair, and he asked, "Dad, do you know what happened to my decoy off of the mantel?"

Grandpa said, "Yes."

Dad said, "What happened to it?"

Grandpa said, "It was wrong, son. You'll get it back. It's not hurt."

"What was wrong?" Dad asked Grandpa.

"There are several things wrong, son, "Grandpa said. "You all were wrong when you told me not to hunt with my old Parker double barrel because it was too valuable to hunt with. That is the finest handling shotgun in the world and you would have it stay in the gun safe. And you all were wrong to leave the beagles in the pen last rabbit season when they should have been running. They have a big heart and ask for nothing but to run a rabbit for you, and most days you left them in the dog pen.

"And, son," It looked like the old man was going to get something off of his chest, "Son, it's wrong to have a Big God and not worship him every minute of every day. I know you go to church on Sundays and on Wednesdays, but son, that Big God is worthy of your praise every minute of every day and every night, and then some.

I'll get your decoy back, son," Grandpa said, "It's in the pond."

Dad was about to faint.

Grandpa said, "The decoy is not hurt. It's where it was made to be. I'll bring it back and put it on your mantel again, and every time you pass it, you think about what I said." And Grandpa went back to sleep.

And Grandpa did get the decoy out of the pond and put it back on the mantel.

Grandpa has been gone for ten years now. And every time Dad passes the mantel, he looks at that old decoy, and sometimes he takes it down and holds it.

And sometimes tears come to his eyes and he tries to hide them, and we know he's thinking about Grandpa.

Dad says that when he is rabbit hunting, and the beagles start running the rabbit real hard, and it is coming his way, that old Parker 16 gauge just floats up and aims itself like it had a mind of its own.

And you can look at my Dad and you can tell that he worships the Big God every minute of every day, and we do, too. Because it's just wrong not to.

Chapter Thirty-Six

Dreamer

Grandpa didn't think much of Yankees. He said that if they had much sense, they wouldn't live where it was so cold.

Stephen C. Foster was a Yankee and he was a gifted songwriter. He wrote minstrel songs mostly.

Minstrel songs were the rage in the 1800s. They were sung on stage by white entertainers dressed up and painted black to mimic black people. Such a thing is politically incorrect today, and Grandpa never did approve of it.

Stephen Foster wrote songs about the Deep South when he had never even been to the Deep South. Some of his minstrel songs, like *Swanee River* and *My Old Kentucky Home*, crossed over into popular music and are recognized as great songs today.

Stephen Foster fell into alcoholism and debt, and shortly before his death, God gave him a song that eclipsed all of his other songs, and even eclipsed most songs ever written by anyone, even to the present day. That song is *Beautiful Dreamer*.

When Grandpa and Grandma met and fell in love, their favorite song was *Beautiful Dreamer*.

When they married, they could only afford the basic necessities, except for one thing. They bought a used Victrola, which played seventy-eight R.P.M. records, and a seventy-eight R.P.M. record of *Beautiful Dreamer*.

Many times over the years when we would drop by unannounced to visit Grandpa and Grandma, we would hear *Beautiful Dreamer* playing on the old Victrola, and we would know that it was an inconvenient time to visit. The old seventy-eight recording of

Beautiful Dreamer became scratchy and worn-out over the years.

For Grandpa and Grandma's fiftieth wedding anniversary, we bought them a sound system with a radio and a stereo record player that would play forty-five R.P.M. records and thirty-three and a third R.P.M. records. And we bought them a new recording of *Beautiful Dreamer*.

They thanked us and made a big fuss about how much they liked the new record player and the new record, but sometimes when we visited unannounced, the old Victrola would be playing the old scratchy *Beautiful Dreamer* recording.

We didn't say anything about it because we knew that old people have their favorite song and versions of songs, just like young people do.

When Grandma died, Grandpa was very sad. He was at the church early for the funeral, and sat on the front pew close to Grandma's casket and he just couldn't stop crying.

As people started gathering into the church, soft music started playing in the background. I could barely hear it, and it wasn't a hymn. It was the old scratchy version of *Beautiful Dreamer*.

Grandma had secretly asked the pastor to have the old record played for Grandpa at the beginning of her funeral, should she die before Grandpa. And she did die before Grandpa, and the preacher moved the old Victrola to the church and played the old record that Grandma requested.

I looked at Grandpa as he slowly recognized the old song. His head came up, and his old stooped back straightened in the pew, and his shoulders quit shaking with sobs. I couldn't see his face, but I suspect that the tears quit falling from his eyes, unless they were tears of joy, as he was transported back over nearly seventy years, to a time long gone.

I don't care if Stephen Foster was a Yankee, God loved him anyway and so do I.

Chapter Thirty-Seven
Grandpa's Buck

Grandpa first saw the buck on the island, when it was a yearling.

Grandpa had a stand, high up in a huge swamp white oak that dominated the small island. Grandpa said that the big yearling buck fed on acorns below his stand for over fifteen minutes, and never knew Grandpa was up above in his stand.

Grandpa said that the buck had a nice rack for a yearling. It had eight regular points and one drop tine on the left beam. Grandpa passed the buck up, because he didn't shoot yearlings.

Yearling bucks are the easiest kind of deer to kill. Their mothers look after them until they get old enough to breed. Then the mother doe chases the yearling buck out of her territory to prevent inbreeding.

The yearling bucks wander around looking for a new territory and they are easy prey for hunters, because they don't yet know the new territory and they are used to being protected by their mother.

Grandpa said that this big yearling buck would make a good trophy in a couple of years, if he lived.

A year later, during hunting season, Grandpa saw the buck again. Grandpa was in the stand, high in the swamp white oak, when he heard the big deer walking in the shallow water towards the island. Grandpa got a good look at the big buck's rack before it sensed his presence and bolted off. Grandpa estimated that at two and one-half years old the buck's antler spread was close to twenty inches. The drop tine was over four inches long.

Whitetail bucks shed their antlers every Spring, and grow a new set by Fall. Genetics supply the blueprint for the antlers. Age and nutrition provide the size.

By the following hunting season, the big buck was three and one-half years old. He was reclusive and evasive, and almost entirely nocturnal in nature. His massive antlers spread twenty-four inches, and the drop tine was six inches long, and flattened on the end, like a shovel.

The buck had learned to circle down wind of the island before he came close enough for Grandpa to get a shot.

Grandpa put up a second stand out over the water, downwind of the island, and from the new stand, Grandpa almost intercepted the buck as it came in down wind. But, as luck would have it, a temporary shift in the wind betrayed Grandpa, and the buck vanished.

By the next hunting season, the buck was four and one-half years old. His massive rack was truly a trophy fit to be mounted. The buck's sixth sense was developed to the point that he sensed danger well before he could smell, hear, or see it. He was nearly impossible to kill. He left plenty of sign on the island, and was there often, but never when Grandpa was there.

When the buck was five and one-half years old, Grandpa's health had failed a little. He had fallen going down his back porch steps and Grandma had made him promise not to get up in any tree stand again. Grandpa was eighty years old that season, and his balance wasn't as good as it once was. So Grandpa sat on the ground at the base of the big swamp white oak. He would lay his big buffalo rifle across his lap, and we think that he napped for most of the hunt.

Because Grandpa was asleep, the big buck's sixth sense didn't detect any danger, and he made the mistake of coming onto the island to eat acorns. The sound of acorns popping as the buck chewed on them, woke Grandpa up and he and the huge buck looked eye to eye, then before Grandpa could raise the big rifle, the buck vanished.

Grandpa had shot many deer with the big rifle. It was a Browning high wall single shot in 45/70 Govt. caliber.

Grandpa's trademark was one shot, behind the shoulder, one dead deer, very little meat spoiled.

One day I had asked Grandpa, "Why don't you get a bolt action,

Grandpa? You might need a second shot sometime."

Grandpa said, "This gun will shoot as many times as I want it to."

I thought he meant that he always got his deer with one shot, until one time a deer bolted as he pulled the trigger, and he thought he had wounded it, so he took two more shots at the deer running through the swamp. He killed the deer with the third shot.

I was listening to the three closely spaced shots, and I thought someone with an automatic or a bolt-action rifle had fired the shots.

Grandpa carried his extra cartridges in a sleeve on his rifle stock, and he could reload and fire aimed shots nearly as fast as if he had a bolt action or auto-loading rifle.

The term 'single shot' is misleading to people who don't know any better. And don't think that a 45/70 is a short-range cartridge.

Grandpa hand-loaded a special bullet, and he loaded hot. His bullets were accurate at long range. His rifle was topped with a Leupold 2X8 variable power scope, and Grandpa could probably outshoot most other deer hunters with their fancy magnum rifles.

But the big buck didn't wait around to find out.

The next year the buck was already on the island feeding when Grandpa waded across before daylight. The buck slipped out his escape route, and was long gone by daylight.

The big buck was in his prime, and was unkillable, for all practical purposes. His huge rack would score well up in the *Boone and Crockett Record Book,* even though the drop tine did not help the score.

The next year the huge buck visited the island again while Grandpa sat under the tree. At seven and one-half years old, the buck was majestic.

No one knows why the buck stood there and let Grandpa raise the big buffalo rifle. Grandpa's eyes were failing, but through the scope, he could see the crosshairs settle just behind the massive shoulder.

Grandpa didn't cock the hammer, and he didn't pull the trigger. He lowered the rifle to his lap and watched the big buck eat his fill of acorns. And then with a glance toward Grandpa the buck silently left the island.

When I came to get Grandpa to help him back across the water because he had been having a hard time walking by himself, he said his knee was hurting.

I said, "From what, Grandpa?"

He said, "From trying to kick myself in the behind." And he told me about letting the big deer go.

Between that deer season and the next season, Grandma died. When deer season came around, Grandpa said he didn't want to go hunting. Dad and I told him that we needed him to go with us. And it was true, we did need him.

On opening morning, I helped Grandpa across the shallow water to the island. He put his arm over my shoulder, and I put my arm around his waist, and we made it across okay. I was surprised at how light he was. I made a mental note to tell Mom so she could make sure he was eating like he was supposed to.

Grandpa leaned up against his favorite tree, and I told him that I would be back at ten a.m..

He said, "Good luck."

The old buck came to the island. The first thing that it did was go check Grandpa's tree, and sure enough, Grandpa was there asleep.

The buck was past his prime now. His antlers were still widespread, but the points were short, and not big around. The drop point was still evident, but it was a chalky white color. The buck's hipbones protruded a little, and he had a few fresh scars and scrapes where younger bucks had chased him away from their potential does.

Grandpa woke up while the old buck was eating acorns and they watched each other for a while. Grandpa didn't raise his big rifle and the old buck never sensed any danger from Grandpa.

The buck was still there when I came to get Grandpa. I caught a glimpse of his old mossy rack as he left out ahead of me. That was the last time that we saw him.

I helped Grandpa up and asked him if he wanted me to carry his rifle. I never really thought that he would let anybody carry his big rifle, but he said, "Yes." And handed the gun to me.

Grandpa said' "I never realized how heavy that big rifle is until now."

I checked to see if the rifle was loaded. It wasn't, and it hadn't been.

When we got back to the truck, Dad asked me, "How was your hunt, son?"

I answered with the phrase that Grandpa had always answered with for as long as I had known him. "Another successful hunt, Dad," I said.

Dad said, "Me, too."

Grandpa said, "Me, too."

A non-hunter might ask, "How could a hunt be successful if nobody killed anything?"

But hunters hunt to have hunted. Sometimes they kill something, but often they don't. The joy of the hunt is in the hunting.

P.S.

A non-hunter might ask the legitimate question: "Why don't you hunt with a camera instead of a gun?"

Hunting with a camera is certainly an option, and people should make the choice that satisfies them.

I might ask: "Would you rather play in a football game, or take a picture of a football game?

Would you rather run in a marathon and cross the finish line, or watch a marathon and take a picture of a runner crossing the finish line?"

Camera hunting does not present the same challenges that gun hunting does. Camera hunters do not have to abide by hunting seasons and hunting regulations. And they don't have to compete against other hunters.

Whitetail deer have a rapid reproduction capacity. In the absence of large carnivores, whitetail deer will quickly overpopulate their environment. Overpopulation will permanently damage the ability of the forest to support deer and other wildlife by completely removing certain species of forage plants from the forest.

In addition, overpopulation of whitetail deer creates an

undesirable and even dangerous interaction between deer and humans. Sport hunting is the only humane, cost-effective way to prevent whitetail deer overpopulation.

Chapter Thirty-Eight
The Chair

Every day when my little cousin got home from school, she would run to the workshop to see my Grandpa. She would say, "Grandpa, let's go feed the fish."

There was a pond in the woods behind the house and a little pier there that they could walk out on and feed Grandpa's catfish. They were tame fish and came to eat when Grandpa banged on the pier, unless a stranger was with him. The fish could see up out of the water somehow, and they wouldn't come up unless it was somebody that they trusted. Nobody caught the fish because they were pets.

On the way to the pond, Grandpa and my cousin walked on a path through the woods. She held onto Grandpa's hand because she was just a little girl at the time. Grandpa would point at a deer track and say, "What's that?"

My cousin would say, "A deer track."

Or he would show her a plant and say what it was, like Birdsfoot Trefoil. The next day he'd show her the plant again and say, "What's that?"

My cousin would say, "Birdsfoot Trefoil." And Grandpa would grin. Grandpa never laughed out loud, but when he grinned, you knew he was happy.

Grandpa didn't talk much and because of that people thought he was unfriendly. But we knew better.

One day Grandpa and my cousin were walking along the old path to the pond and she noticed an old rocking chair leaning up against a tree on a little hill not far from the path.

"What's that chair doing out there, Grandpa? " she asked.

"Well, " he said, "I put it out there. It's broken."

"Can't you fix it, Grandpa?" my cousin asked. She knew he fixed lots of things like that in his shop.

It's just too old, sweetheart," he said. "I fixed it a long time ago after some rich folks threw it away. I put a new rocker on it and tightened all the joints. I used it for over fifty years on the front porch. It was made out of good, stout hickory."

"Why don't you fix it again?" she asked.

Grandpa said, "It's worn out, brittle. It can't be fixed any more."

"Why did you put it out here?" she asked.

"Most people would throw it in the dump," he said. "But it deserved better than that, so I brought it back out here where it belonged and set it by that old hickory tree."

"I believe its grinning, Grandpa," my cousin said.

I think Grandpa was grinning, too. Those rich folks weren't as rich as my Grandpa in things that matter.

Chapter Thirty-Nine
The Birthday Party

My little niece invited Grandpa to her birthday party on her fifth birthday, and Grandpa said he would be there, and Grandpa grew up in a time when if you said you were going to do something, you did it.

But on the day of the party, Grandpa couldn't find a ride to my niece's house, twenty-five miles away. Grandpa's drivers license and the keys to his old truck had been taken away when he got feeble and his eyesight failed. Dad had to work that day, and Mom was gone to a church meeting out of town. And I was off on an all day fishing trip with my brother.

So Grandpa wrapped the little praying man that he had carved for my niece in brown paper and put it in his pocket and set out walking. Or, more like shuffling. Grandpa couldn't walk by himself anymore. His big old dog walked by his side and Grandpa steadied himself on the dog everywhere he went.

My niece was playing in the yard with her little friends when she saw Grandpa coming. The party was almost over. With tears of joy in her eyes, she hollered, "Papa, I knew you would come, I just knew it! I saved you some ice cream and cake."

A little while later the police came roaring up, and my dad came roaring up. Dad told my brother's wife, "The old man is missing. We've got to find him!"

Brother's wife said, "He's not missing. He's sitting in the house eating his third helping of ice cream and birthday cake."

"Thank, God," said my dad. "How'd he get here?"

She said, "He walked. He just came walking up, leaning on that big old wolf dog, and it growling at everybody."

My Dad went into the house and up to the table where Grandpa was eating ice cream and cake. "I love you, old man," Dad said. "How'd you get here?"

"Walked," Grandpa said.

"Old man, it's over twenty-five miles from our house to here," Dad said.

"Not the way I came," Grandpa said. "It's barely over five miles if you come through the swamp."

Now, Grandpa was a retired forester, and the big swamp didn't scare him like it does most people. He wasn't afraid of snakes and he never got lost.

Grandpa said, "I found some good buck sign in the middle of that old swamp, and come deer season I'm going back in there and kill me a big buck."

My dad said, "Dad, when you do go back in the swamp deer hunting, please wear something other than that old bathrobe and those flimsy bedroom slippers that you wore this time."

Chapter Forty
Suppertime

They wouldn't let Grandpa drive because of his eyesight, and he was sort of feeble after Grandma died. So he asked me to take him on a little errand that he needed to run.

When I picked him up at Mom and Dad's, he laid an old garden hoe in the back of my pickup truck and then slowly got in and shut the door.

Grandpa directed me to drive down the Old Swamp Road for a couple of miles, then we turned off on a narrow abandoned side road for a mile or so. When we got to the end of the side road, we stopped the truck and got out.

Grandpa picked up the hoe and started down a dim path for quite a ways, until up ahead I saw a little shanty house built out over the water of an old boat road which was probably cleaned out years ago when the virgin cypress was logged.

As we approached the house, I could see that it had been long abandoned, although it was in good shape to be so old. It was built out of the heartwood of cypress. Cypress sapwood will rot away like pine, but cypress heartwood will last a long, long time.

Grandpa said, "Watch your step, son," as we walked across the plank leading up to the door.

We went in, and the little one room house was empty except for some built-in furniture, like bunks, and shelves. Grandpa went through to the other door, and then out onto a small deck over the water.

Grandpa said, pointing at the water, "You can catch some good sun perch and mud cats right here."

Grandpa went back in the house and said, "This room sure seems small. In my memory, it seems so big."

He tried to climb the peg ladder to the sleeping loft, but he couldn't, so I did.

"There's nothing up here, Grandpa," I said.

"I know it," he said.

Grandpa went to every corner of the room, and examined everything. Then he reached up in the rafters over the doorway, and from a small cavity he withdrew an old worn-out pocketknife. Its blades were worn down narrow, and it had one missing handle replaced with lead.

Grandpa handed the knife to me and said, "This is your Great Grandpa's pocket knife. Take care of it, and pass it on to whichever of your children or grandchildren that you know will cherish it and take good care of it."

Grandpa kept looking at the fireplace as if he saw something there. All I could see was the old cooking iron that swiveled out on the side of the fireplace to hang the cooking pots on over the fire. But Grandpa went over by the fireplace, and I heard him mumble, "It's suppertime."

Then Grandpa went out of the cabin and back across the plank walkway to the dirt pathway. Then he followed a dim side pathway that led to a small knoll, called a hummock around here, which was a short way from the cabin.

On the top of the little knoll were two grave markers made out of cypress heartwood. On one it said, "Father," and on the other it said "Mother." And nearby were four cypress crosses, and on two of the crosses it said "Baby Girl," and on two it said "Baby Boy."

Grandpa began to hoe the weeds from around the grave markers, and he didn't offer to let me help. And every once in a while, he would mop his face with his shirtsleeve. He wasn't sweating so much as crying. But I didn't intrude.

Finally he knelt at each grave and prayed.

Then Grandpa got to his feet and handed the hoe to me, and Grandpa said, "In my will I'm leaving this little place to you because

I know that you will cherish it and do what's right. Now let's go home, it's Suppertime."

At Grandpa's funeral, they sang the beautiful old hymn "Suppertime" by Ira F. Stanphill. And everybody cried and cried.

Chapter Forty-One
Me and this Old Dog

My aunt was in the kitchen fixing supper. She heard the vehicle pull up outside and my uncle was home. She said, "Better check on your dad, he left in his old truck this morning with that old dog and his old rifle."

My uncle said, "How did he start the truck? The battery was down and it hasn't been run in years since the doctor made him quit driving. How did the old dog get up in the truck? He couldn't get up the porch steps to eat his food. He must have gone to our hunting spot in the swamp. I told him to wait until I got home and I'd go with him. I'll drive out there and make sure he's okay." My uncle left in a hurry, more worried than he let on.

Uncle drove the several miles to the swamp talking to himself, "Don't that beat all. That old man can't see well enough to drive. What are we going to do if he keeps running off?"

Uncle reached the end of the old swamp road. Sure enough, there was the old truck. Uncle said, "Where's Dad and that dog. Surely they didn't try to walk the trail across the beaver dam to the island. That's a long hard walk for a young man. In several places, the water is knee deep."

The old swamp buck slipped across the small island. He came to a cautious stop, realizing that he was in the same spot where the old man had caught him dead-to-rights a year ago, and the year before that. The huge buck looked between the splayed roots of the aged swamp oak and sure enough the old man was there, but as in previous years, he didn't raise the big single shot that had accounted for so many of the buck's ancestors.

The buck's sixth sense detected no danger from the old man or from the huge dog lying at his feet. Hearing a faint noise from the direction of the beaver dam, the old buck faded away like a ghost in the dim swamp.

Still fussing continuously, my uncle made it across the beaver dam, wet to the knees in swamp water and black muck. He saw the old man in his favorite spot at the foot of the huge oak. "At least he didn't try to climb into the high stand like he used to," he fussed.

"Dad," my uncle called.

No answer, except a low growl from the dog. The dog had been his dad's constant companion ever since his dad found the week-old pup, many years ago, abandoned with no hope of reaching food or water by some thoughtless person. That was the only time in my uncle's life that he had heard his dad use profanity.

"Dad," my uncle called.

The dog growled again. The dog knew the old man was gone, but he had left his things here at the base of this tree, so the dog would stay here and guard them until he got back.

The big 'buff' rifle, the familiar old clothes, and the worn-out frame of a body that the old man had occupied were here, so the dog would stay, period.

"Dad," my uncle called, but he knew his best friend was gone.

"Come on, old dog. Let's go get help," he said, and turned back toward the beaver dam, but the dog wouldn't move. My uncle took a few more steps and then fell to his knees. For several minutes, great sobs convulsed his slumped shoulders.

After a long while he raised his hands toward heaven and said "Lord, I know Dad is happier now than at any time since Mom died, but me and this old dog…"

Chapter Forty-Two
The Flintlock

My little sister called him "Papa", but Daddy called him the "Old Man." It made her mad back then, but now she knows "Old Man" was a term of respect.

Grandpa stayed in his workshop all day, most every day. My sister would go in there as much as Daddy would let her. Grandpa would reach out and shake her hand when she came in. It made her feel big, even though she was just a small wisp of a girl. The top of sister's head was lower than the top of Grandpa's workbench. His big hand always surprised her. It felt like wood and she always thought, "What if he squeezed and crushed my hand?" But she knew he never would.

Sister never let Grandpa get away with just a handshake. She always made him bend down so she could hug his neck and kiss him on the cheek. Grandpa always greeted her with one word, "Punkin."

If he talked, she didn't understand much he said, and I don't think he understood much of what sister said either, but that didn't matter.

Grandpa always turned the radio down when sister came into his shop. He listened to *American Family Radio* all day long, every day, and it was usually turned up pretty loud. He wore a big magnifying visor to work at his workbench. Every once in a while he would take it off, put a few scraps of wood in the little homemade wood stove and sit in his rocking chair.

Sometimes Grandpa would just sit for a long time, and sometimes he would talk to that big old dog that always slept by the stove. The dog never talked back, but I think it listened. Sister didn't ever go near the big old dog because he growled at everybody except

Grandpa.

The only time the old dog ever moved was when Grandpa went in the house and the dog would follow to the back porch and lay by the door.

Grandpa had a picture of Grandma out there and we often saw him holding it. Sister never knew Grandma, but she could see from the picture that Grandma was a handsome, happy-looking woman, with snow-white hair piled up on her head in the Pentecostal way.

Mama told us that Grandma played the piano and sang in the choir in the same church we go to. Mom said Grandma had the voice of an angel.

Daddy said Grandpa was making guns in his shop, and not to touch any of his tools, because they were razor sharp and Grandpa knew exactly where each tool was supposed to be, so don't move any.

One day when we came home from school, Grandpa was not in the shop. Mama said he went to stay with Grandma. Daddy stayed gone in the woods for a long time. When he finally came home, he wouldn't talk to anybody except Mama. It worried us.

One day Daddy went out to Grandpa's shop and sat in Grandpa's chair talking to the old dog for a long time. Mama said the old dog wouldn't eat.

When Daddy came out of Grandpa's shop, he handed my little sister something wrapped up in an old blanket. It was twice as long as she was tall and it felt heavy.

She carefully laid it on the floor and unwrapped the blanket. Grandpa hadn't been making guns in the shop! He had been making the most beautiful flintlock rifle in the world, and on a flat place on the top of the barrel it said, "FOR PUNKIN."

Chapter Forty-Three
The Old Dog

The phone rang. It was my Dad. He said, "You need to come over here and do something with your Grandpa's old dog. He still won't eat."

Grandpa died about a month ago, and the old dog took it pretty hard. Grandpa and the dog had been companions for many years. I was just a boy when Grandpa brought the dog home. He was just a little pup that someone had abandoned on the roadside. Grandpa fed him with a bottle until he got big enough to drink milk out of a dish.

The pup grew up fast and looked to me like a huge wolf. He was mostly black with blue spots, and had one glass eye. Grandpa said that he suspected the pup came from a farm down the road, where the farmer had a big male Husky and a female Catahoula Cur.

The big dog had a name but Grandpa just called him "Dog." Dog wouldn't tolerate anybody but Grandpa. He would growl at everybody else. If anybody came into the yard, Dog would stand in between him or her and Grandpa. He never bit anybody, but I can't imagine that anybody would be foolish enough to try and get past him.

Dog would tolerate little toddlers to a point. Dad said that one day my baby sister, just starting to walk, wandered out toward the road. Dog hooked one huge fang through the strap of her little overalls and guided her back to the house. And sometimes in Grandpa's workshop, sister would curl up against Dog and take a nap.

Grandpa worked in his shop every day, doing woodcarvings and making flintlock rifles. Then Grandma died and Grandpa started getting feeble like. He still went to his workshop every day, but he didn't work much. He would sit in his rocker by the little wood stove and talk to Dog.

Dog always looked at Grandpa's face and listened to what Grandpa said. And he understood Grandpa.

In the morning, Dog would sit by the back door until Grandpa came out and walk beside Grandpa to the workshop. Grandpa couldn't walk well by himself and had to lean on the big dog. Then Grandpa would sit in his big rocker and listen to the Gospel station on the radio. And Dog would curl up by the wood stove until time to take Grandpa back to the house.

Mom would bring Grandpa a big plate of food at lunchtime, and Grandpa would pick around on it some and then give it to Dog. Dog's favorite thing was table scraps. Mom knew who really got the food, but she never said anything.

Then about a month ago, Grandpa died, and Dog quit eating. I went over there when Dad called and took Dog a big plate of leftovers that Mom fixed for him. And I sat down in Grandpa's rocker and turned on the Gospel music station and I talked to Dog for a long time. But Dog wouldn't eat.

I didn't cry when Grandpa died. Grown men don't cry. I hadn't cried since I was a child, but for some reason tears started pouring out of my eyes and didn't stop until I was cried empty.

Dog moved around and laid his big head on my foot, and his tail thumped the floor a couple of times. It seems like we sat that way for hours.

Finally I had to go home. Dog never did eat. Now he's with Grandpa, I'm sure. God sometimes forges a bond that is stronger than death. It's called "Love."

Chapter Forty-Four
Christmas

Grandma had sung in the choir ever since she was the youngest member at fourteen years old. She had a high, clear, perfect voice, and people said that she sang like an angel.

Because Grandma was a Pentecostal, her hair had never been cut. It was a beautiful, light brown in color, and fell to below her waist.

At Christmas time, when our church had special music, people came from miles around to see and hear the musical, and some came especially to hear Grandma sing.

As Grandma got older, her voice became more mellow. She always expressed a lot of feeling and worship when she sang and before her song was over, the whole congregation would be standing, and raising their hands towards heaven.

Grandpa liked the old favorite hymns, so those were what Grandma sang most of the time.

All of a sudden, it seemed to Grandma, she was the oldest member of the choir.

The pastor recruited a new music director. And to tell the truth, he was the most extraordinarily gifted person our church had ever had. He was dedicated to worship and could play the keyboard and sing as beautifully as anybody who ever got on *The Grand Old Opry.*

The new music director liked modern songs, and the younger members of the choir liked modern songs, and so did the congregation.

The younger girls and ladies mostly wore their hair down, but the elderly ladies like Grandma wore their hair up. Both ways are beautiful.

Grandma had a fight with cancer and God cured her, but the

chemotherapy made her beautiful hair that had never been cut, fall out. Grandma took it in stride, like she did everything else, but I think it made her feel self-conscious to be in the choir, before the church, with her wig, and then with her short hair growing back.

The preacher told her not to worry, but I could tell that Grandma was slowly turning her place in the choir over to the younger people.

We always had our family reunion on Christmas Eve and it was always a full house at Grandpa and Grandma's.

Grandpa always demanded a wholly religious Christmas. He wouldn't even have had a Christmas tree if Grandma hadn't insisted on one. So Grandpa would always find a cedar or a short leaf pine in the pasture and bring it in, and Grandma would decorate it. And the tree always smelled so good.

And we would all eat a big Christmas meal together.

We didn't exchange gifts at the Christmas reunion because of Grandpa's request not to commercialize Christmas.

After the meal somebody would always find Grandpa's old guitar and bring it to him.

Grandpa couldn't sing. It is said that he couldn't carry a tune in a bucket. And he only knew one song on his guitar.

Grandpa was stubborn. Everybody admits that. One time he jokingly said that if you're stubborn enough, you don't have to be right.

Grandpa got his guitar a long time ago, and was determined to learn how to play at least one song on it. And he finally did. He learned how to play "Wildwood Flower."

"Wildwood Flower" is an old folk song that was passed down orally from back in the 1800s. It was first recorded by the Carter Family in 1927. The Carter Family recorded the folk version that used archaic words and phrases, and doesn't totally make sense to us now, but it is beautiful.

Just like the King James Version of the *Bible*. There are many modern versions of the *Bible* that are technically more correct than the Kings James Version, but they are not as beautiful.

The King James Version of the *Bible* was purposely written to read like beautiful poetry, and with God's inspiration, it does read like beautiful poetry.

When Grandpa started playing "Wildwood Flower," Grandma would move over by him and sing. And she would sing the folk version. And it was so beautiful.

Then one year Grandma passed away. And at our reunion that year, nobody brought Grandpa's guitar out to him. We were afraid it would be too hard on him to play with Grandma gone.

Then the next year Grandpa passed away.

When we had our Christmas reunion, of course it wasn't the same.

At the meal, everybody picked around on the food and said how good it was, but nobody was hungry. We had an artificial Christmas tree. It was white, and it didn't smell like anything. We drew names and exchanged gifts. And then just sat around.

Somebody went and got Grandpa's guitar and handed it to my cousin. Cousin could sure enough play a guitar. He even played in a small local band. Cousin strummed a few chords, and then started playing "Wildwood Flower." One of my other cousins got up and went and stood by him and started singing.

She sung the old folk version of "Wildwood Flower," and her voice was as pretty and clear as an angel. Her beautiful long hair, that had never been cut, was longer than her waist.

After the first verse, my Dad stood up and bowed his head, and by the time the song was finished everybody else was standing, and there wasn't a dry eye in the house.

Dad went and got a big empty box and sat it by the Christmas tree. And he put the gift that he had received into the box. And everybody else there, even the little kids, put their gifts into the big box.

That night we all went to the Christmas Eve program at our little church, and we left the box of gifts with the other donations for less fortunate people. We listened to the beautiful program that the music director had put together. It included all the old favorite Christmas songs plus beautiful new songs, too.

We celebrated the Birth of the Precious Baby, Jesus the Christ. And we knew that Grandpa and Grandma approved.

Chapter Forty-Five
The Preacher

My uncle, my Dad's oldest brother, is a preacher. He lives several states away, and we rarely saw him before Grandpa died. Uncle drove in just in time for Grandpa's funeral and was planning to leave the following morning. But when he got into his car to leave, the car wouldn't start.

It was a beautiful luxury car, made in Germany, and probably worth more than our whole farm, I bet. Trouble is, nobody within a hundred miles could work on that kind of car. And it was Saturday so nobody was available until Monday.

Now Uncle was always in a hurry. Every year he would promise Grandpa that he would come for Thanksgiving or Christmas and that they would go rabbit hunting or deer hunting together like they used to. But when the time came, Uncle would call and say he was preaching or teaching somewhere that week and he wouldn't be able to come visit Grandpa. Grandpa always said that he understood, and that preaching was more important than visiting.

Uncle was quite famous in the Church, so when he got held over because of car trouble, our little church asked him to speak to us on Sunday. And Uncle said he would.

On Saturday, he went rabbit hunting with my Dad, and they got to telling funny stories about Grandpa, and repeating some of Grandpa's old corny jokes, and they got to laughing and they laughed until they cried. When they came home, their eyes were all red, but their hearts were back in the right place.

On Sunday, Uncle gave the sermon in our church. His sermons were well known to run from long to very, very long. Some people said that Uncle liked to hear himself preach.

After our preacher got the preliminaries out of the way, he introduced Uncle and turned the service over to him.

Uncle stepped behind the lectern said, "God is more important than anything else. Yes, even more important than everything else put together. God chose the Father-Son relationship to demonstrate the most important event that has ever occurred. And with that event God provided your way to everlasting life. But I have found that there is something else that is more important than running all over the world preaching long sermons all the time. God wrote in stone with his own finger, "Honor Thy Father and Thy Mother."

Uncle continued, "If only I could have the chance to make up those visits to my mom and dad that I promised to make but canceled because I thought I was too busy."

Then Uncle began to cry, and he sat down without saying anything else.

On Monday morning, the mechanic came from the big city a long way away. When he tried to start Uncle's car, it started perfectly. The mechanic tried it several times and then said, "There's nothing wrong with this car."

So Uncle went back to his home. But now he comes to see us several times a year, always during hunting season, of course. And he and Dad always get to laughing and telling stories about Grandpa.

Chapter Forty-Six
The Tree

It was the opening morning of the first deer season after Grandpa died and I didn't feel like going hunting. It was like the magic had died. I think Dad felt the same way. He just wasn't enthusiastic about opening morning like he used to be.

Hunting is a family tradition with us, and Grandpa had always been part of it. Now Grandpa was gone and everything seemed different.

But I felt that it was my responsibility to go, so Dad would go. He had taken Grandpa's loss very hard and he needed to get back to normal, and hunting is what was normal.

So we arrived at the place on the edge of the Big Swamp where we usually park the truck and Dad said that he would go to his usual stand.

I told Dad that I guess I would go to the stand in the big cow oak on Grandpa's island. It was Grandpa's favorite spot. He had died leaning up against the big tree, with his big buffalo rifle resting across his lap and his big dog lying at his feet.

I forced myself to take the path to the island. I had to wade shallow water most of the way.

I made my way back to the center of the little island where the big swamp white oak, we call them cow oaks, had dominated the island for well over one hundred years.

But in the early dawn I could see a huge opening in the forest canopy. The monster cow oak was lying on the ground amidst the wreckage of several smaller trees that it had crushed when it fell. Wind had blown it over. There was a huge cavity in the ground where the roots had torn loose.

It took a while for my mind to accept the fact that the landmark was gone. The tree had always seemed so immortal, just like Grandpa had.

I sat on the tree trunk for a long while and thought about Grandpa and about his favorite tree, and I cried some. Out of self-pity, I guess.

Finally, I began to be aware of my surroundings again, and I noticed how beautiful the island was. I saw that deer had been feeding on acorns and I saw a wild turkey tail feather.

And as I began to notice things again, I saw hundreds of tiny cow oak seedlings that had sprouted in the opening left by the giant tree when it fell.

At the appointed time, I went back to the truck. Dad was already there. He said that he hadn't seen any deer, but that he saw a good bit of deer sign. I told Dad about the big tree and about the seedlings taking its place. He didn't say anything.

Dad's eyes were red. I think he was okay, and that he was glad that we had come. We rode home mostly in silence.

When we got to my house and got out of the truck, my little five-year-old son ran out all excited, carrying his little wooden popgun.

My little son said, "Grandpa, when do I get to go hunting with you? Please take me, please!"

I looked at my Dad. His eyes came to life. The magic was back.

One generation passeth away, and another generation cometh. (Ecclesiastes 1:4)

Chapter Forty-Seven
The Tractor

The old tractor never missed a tick for my brother. It never failed to start, never broke down, and never quit until he turned it off. He mowed the church property with it, and mowed a few grown-up lots around town when people asked him to. I doubt he ever got paid, or for that matter, ever asked for pay. He had the old tractor for a long time.

Brother had a good childhood, good family guidance and support. The VietNam war broke out, and Brother went, and was wounded twice. The Devil stepped in and changed Brother's outlook on life.

The second wound probably would have killed him, but the Devil needed a few good men, and Brother survived, although with a limp he would never outgrow.

Brother got a steady job when he came home from the war, but on paydays he'd stop at the bar, and when he finally left, the paycheck would be gone. The Devil loved the cycle of whisky, cigarettes, profanity, and not just a little spousal abuse.

Sister-in-law would iron clothes for the neighbors, with the two little ones hanging on her skirt. Cornbread soaked in milk was a feast to them.

'But the Devil made a big mistake. He put Brother up to going into the little Pentecostal church one Sunday, and dragging Sister-in-law and the kids out in front of everybody. It didn't work like the Devil wanted. What happened was, God slew Brother, in the Spirit, right in front of everybody.

When Brother finally got up from the altar, he asked for forgiveness of his sins, was baptized by submergence in water, and was filled with the Holy Spirit on the spot. He was reborn a clean man, with a clean record, and he stayed clean, and is clean in Heaven today.

That's not to say he wasn't a bit eccentric. But aren't we all? He always had a touch of Napoleon's Syndrome; Short Peoples' Complex. He was five feet two inches tall and tried to compensate for being short in small ways that were abrasive to some, but not to me. I guess he liked me. I liked him.

But the Devil got real mad when God kicked him out of Brother. And the Devil jumped into that old tractor.

Brother passed away, and Sister-in-law gave the tractor to me because I asked to buy it, and she knew I needed it to make food plots on the hunting lease.

When I went to Sister-in-law's to get the tractor, it wouldn't start, so I tried to jump it off, but it caught on fire. Not much damage, just wires and such. When I got the fire put out, I used a hand wench to pull it up on the trailer. That's when I discovered the problem with the trailer hitch that would let the trailer seesaw up in front from the weight of the tractor on the back. Not much of a problem unless the tailgate was down. A vee-shaped tailgate cannot be repaired.

I did get the tractor as far as the tractor repair shop. It hadn't started because it needed a battery and a starter. New battery, new starter, points, plugs, condenser, and coil, and the tractor runs good. But the battery won't charge. New alternator, new voltage regulator, now the tractor comes home ready to work.

On the first turn around, the steering wheel broke off. I drove it home with a pair of vice grip pliers clamped onto the steering column. New steering wheel, and then try again. A loud pop and the new steering wheel turns round and round.

I took the tractor back to the repair shop, and the shop foreman says, "We probably can't get these steering gears, but if you're lucky you might find them on some old salvage tractor."

I finally hit a streak of good luck. When the mechanic got into the gears they were okay. It only needed a few gaskets and so forth. When I went to pick up the tractor, the shop foreman asked me, "Did somebody sell you this tractor?"

I said, "No, we inherited it."

He didn't say anything else. He just kept adding up the bill.

The good luck continued and I bought a used bush hog type rotary mower for two hundred dollars. What a bargain. But the first time I used it, the stump jumper and blades fell off. Still, you have to expect repairs to used equipment.

But the welder wouldn't weld the hardened steel shaft, and the ag equipment expert traced the huge bearing box back to 1948 and found out parts haven't been available for years. "It's a good bearing box," he said. "They last for years."

I can still disk the food plots, I thought. So I hooked up the disk. But the tractor was getting hard to shift, and wouldn't shift out of gear.

Throwout bearing and clutch, the mechanic said. "We'll have to split her for that." Split her, in mechanic talk, means to take the tractor in half. Not cheap.

Four months later, I got the call. The tractor was ready. I picked it up, and to celebrate, I bought a new, eighty-nine dollar, cushioned tractor seat, with the remainder of a monthly paycheck.

I unloaded the tractor and put it lovingly under the carport. I installed the beautiful cushioned seat and went into the house to gloat on how persistence always pays off.

An hour or two later, I went to the carport to move the tractor to its private spot in the barn. The eighty-nine dollar tractor seat was shredded. Pieces of foam were all over the yard. The beautiful leather-like cover was hanging in tatters.

The Devil had finally come out of the tractor, but now he was in my yard dog.

Chapter Forty-Eight
Cooking

There were a few things I didn't know when I married CoRenna. Luckily, and by God's will, they turned out to be good things.

Mama and CoRenna both cooked in big, heavy, black iron pots, but their way of cooking was as different as day and night.

Mom put the big pot on the stove with the fire off, and put cold water in the pot, then cut up vegetables and meat, or whatever the ingredients were, and then mixed it all up, and then turned the fire on. The food all cooked together, and was delicious, if somewhat bland.

But we all liked bland, and bland is easy on our digestive systems.

Mom fixes peas and cornbread with every meal, year around.

In north Louisiana, people don't ask, "How's your garden doing?" They ask, "How are your peas doing?"

CoRenna's staple is rice three or more times a day.

CoRenna puts the big pot on the stove empty, and then turns on the fire. When the pot starts smoking, CoRenna adds a couple of things and makes a roux. Everything she cooks starts with a roux, and a hot pot. The heat required to brown a roux happens to be the heat required to make the chemical changes in food, that provide extraordinary flavors.

CoRenna can cook the same basic meat and vegetables as Mom, but it will taste entirely different.

For spiciness Mom uses bell peppers, sweet banana peppers, and sweet Vidalia onions.

CoRenna uses Jalapeno peppers for her mild cooking. Lord knows where she gets her onions. They will stay with you for a week.

A small bottle of Tabasco sauce lasts Mom for years. CoRenna uses a small bottle of Tabasco sauce on her eggs every morning. She

137

buys it by the case.

Grandma, my Mom, and my sisters are beautiful women, with light brown or blond hair, and light colored eyes, usually blue or green. They are as tall and strong as most men. They are slow to anger, and have much patience. I think they take after our German ancestors. They are kind and sweet, and have much ability to forgive. But they never forget.

And if they get in a fight, they hit with a fist like a man. No slapping, kicking, scratching, or biting. Thank God, they don't get in many fights.

CoRenna is beautiful, with dark eyes and dark hair, and a short fuse. You don't have to wonder what she is thinking; she'll let you know immediately.

When we go to visit CoRenna's folks on the coast, I used to wonder what those big, warehouse looking buildings, with the empty parking lots that would hold several hundred cars, were doing out in the middle of nowhere.

Then CoRenna took me to one on a Friday afternoon, to 'pass a good time', and it was completely different. The parking lot was full, and inside the building were all manner of people, from babies to elderly, and they were dancing to a live local band that sang and played in French.

CoRenna danced until daylight on Saturday morning and then woke me up. I was sleeping on a blanket along the wall with the small children.

CoRenna said, "Let's go fishing." So we went fishing all day, with her dad on his boat.

What we call fish in north Louisiana; they call bait on the coast. The fish we catch in north Louisiana, Mom cooks whole in a frying pan. The fish they catch off the coast, CoRenna cooks in sections that look like sticks of firewood, in the turkey roaster. You cut steaks off of them at the table.

God made the perfect choice when he put CoRenna and me together. She is a wonderful wife and mother. And I can't imagine life without her. Even if it is like being on a roller coaster with a lit firecracker in my hand.

Chapter Forty-Nine
The Island

My youngest sister has been accused of being stingy with words, but that's not true. She's just not wasteful, never uses two syllables when a one-syllable sentence will do.

Dad taught her that, I thought as we sat on the tailgate of the truck waiting for her to return. We were hunting the edge of the Big Swamp and she was a little late. But that wasn't unusual.

She was like Mom; tall, thin, athletic, and deceptively strong, and very pretty. Those pesky boyfriends sure thought so.

I tried to remember when I first noticed the small things that happened as she grew up. Like when the groups she shot with her hand-loads were tighter than those I shot with my hand-loads. And when she started going higher in a tree with her climbing stand than I would go with mine. Or when I realized that her broad-heads were sharper than mine, and her bow was set on a higher power than mine.

But "Ha," she didn't have bursitis in her shoulder like I did. When she was just a baby I picked up the big brass bearing at the welding shop that had never been picked up by one man before. I'm glad that bearing is gone now, because she would probably go into town and lift it. I'd like to keep at least one record for myself.

Two quick college degrees, a good job, and she was doing fine. Then that brother-in-law had to come along.

Oh, he's okay. He's a devoted husband, has a good job, and never misses church. But he'd rather work than hunt. He shoots store-bought ammo in his deer rifle, and he doesn't even own a hunting bow. Well, there's always hope.

We saw her coming with that long, quiet stride. Now days when we walked together, she always led. I had a hard time keeping up, but she never knew it.

She laid her climbing stand on the tailgate and said, "I found the Island." A four-word sentence! I knew she was excited if she was that gabby.

"How?" I asked.

We had been dreaming of finding an island in the big swamp for twenty years, but never had been able to penetrate the muck that was too soft to walk on, but not wet enough to float a boat.

"I climbed a tree on a hill that looked out over the swamp. I saw three big pines out there." she said. She knew that pines wouldn't grow in the water, so there must be dry land out there.

Dad asked, "How can we get out there?"

She answered, "I found a way across the beaver dam, then on a big log over deeper water, then on a ridge, then across more deep water on a log and you're there."

In the swamp, a ridge is any land that sticks up above the water. "How's it look?" I asked.

"Beautiful," she said. "It's never been logged. There's huge swamp white oaks, willow oaks, laurel oaks, water oaks, overcup oaks, and three huge pines, nearly four feet in diameter."

" Any sign?" Dad asked.

"Lots," she said. "It's everywhere. Deer, turkey. I saw droves of squirrels."

We got into the truck. She's not bossy, but she wouldn't start the motor until we fastened our seat belts. I tried to wait her out once, but wasn't successful.

The next morning we arrived at the Big Swamp bright and early, about an hour before sunrise. She wanted to be up in her stand and ready at first light.

"If you get lost, shoot three times every five minutes," I told her. It was a joke, as she never got lost, and anyway she only had five arrows in her bow quiver.

At ten o'clock, Dad and I were back at the truck, waiting on the tailgate. At ten thirty, she still wasn't back. We decided to walk down to the beaver pond and see if we could meet her and walk back with her. When we got within sight of the beaver pond, we saw her skidding a big field-dressed doe out of the pond and onto dry land.

She had her bow in one hand, her climbing stand in the other hand, and was skidding the deer with a rope around her waist and tied to the deer's neck. She was wet and mucky from the waist down. Nodding her head towards the big doe, she said, "Floats good."

"Baby," Dad said, "I wish you'd lay off of some of this stuff, at least until you get through this pregnancy! And please show me the trail into that island!"

Chapter Fifty

The Test

Some things that I know, are facts, and some things that I know, are beliefs.

It is a fact promised by God in the Bible that if a person will accept Jesus as their Savior, truly repent of their sins and vow to try as best they can, not to sin again, and be baptized by submersion by someone with the authority to perform baptism in Jesus' name, then they will be filled with the Holy Spirit of Jesus and will be given Salvation and Eternal Life in Heaven through God's Grace.

The only thing that can prevent the fulfillment of this promise is if the person intentionally rejects or denies Jesus as Savior and Almighty God.

Facts don't change, but beliefs can. When I was very young I believed my Dad was the strongest, smartest person on earth, and that my Mom was the sweetest and most beautiful person on earth. This is still my belief, but I can't prove it to be a fact, and I now realize that other people may think the same of their parents.

It had always been my belief that my Dad was permanently granted salvation by God, and that my Dad's eternal life in Heaven was unquestionable.

But then, one day my mom's doctor told her to come back in and redo her mammogram, that the first one had not been clear.

Mom and Dad had a marriage blessed by God, and they were bonded into one person by God. In some marriages, the husband and wife are on opposite sides. Dad and Mom were always on the same side. They supported each other in public and in private. Dad and Mom's love for each other was an example of the true meaning of love: Love is when you care more for someone else than you do for yourself.

They went to church regularly together, never separately.

Mom's doctor called and said that the second x-ray looked funny also, and she needed to come in again, but not to worry, as it was probably nothing.

After the doctor's examination, he told Mom and Dad that Mom had a small lump in her breast that should be removed for biopsy, but not to worry because ninety-nine per cent of this kind of lump was benign.

We all prayed for God to heal mom, and our church prayed for her at prayer request time.

The lump was removed and the doctor called Mom and Dad in to his office. He said that the lump was a particularly nasty type of cancer, but that he was sure radical surgery, chemotherapy, and radiation would cure it.

We prayed and prayed, and when Mom went into the operating room, our pastor, and Mom's mother, and many other family members, and church family members sat with Dad in the waiting room. We prayed and prayed.

When the surgeon came out he said that Mom came through the operation fine, but that the cancer had spread and would require chemotherapy and radiation.

Dad rarely left Mom's side, and when she was too sick to go to church he wouldn't go without her. When mom's beautiful long hair that had never been cut fell out from the chemotherapy, Dad told her that she was more beautiful than ever, and he wasn't lying. But the constant bad news was wearing Dad down.

Mom didn't finish the six weeks of radiation because God called her home before it was finished.

Dad had always had Grandpa and Grandma to turn to for strength and advice, but they had both passed away several years before.

At Mom's funeral, Dad looked weak and like he had been defeated. Dad never cried in public, but I could tell by looking at his eyes that he had been crying a lot.

The funeral was on Friday and I began to believe that Dad might blame God for Mom's suffering and death. I know that I had serious questions about why God would let Mom suffer and die like she did.

On Sunday morning I called and told Dad that we would pick him up on our way to church.

He said, "No."

It was my belief that he wouldn't go to church without Mom.

We went on to church and went in and sat down. The gathering music was already playing softly. I was very unhappy and worried because life on earth is just a 'tick' of time compared to eternity, and I believed my Dad was rejecting his Salvation for eternity.

Then Dad came in the door and walked straight past where he and Mom usually sat, and he went to the altar and kneeled and started to worship and pray out loud. He thanked God for creating Mom, and for sending her to him, and he thanked God for the wonderful life that they had had together, and he thanked God for taking Mom to Heaven and putting her in a place of honor in the Angel Choir. He said that he understood why God tested his people and chose the very best to stand closest to Him in Heaven. And he asked God to save a place for him by Mom, if it be God's will.

Some things are beliefs and some are facts. It is a fact that Dad's salvation is guaranteed by God just like Mom's is.

Dad passed the test.

Chapter Fifty-One
Brother-in-law

I love my brother-in-law. He's a good provider, highly educated, and a wonderful family man.

I know that you are expecting this next word: But.

But, he's a liberal from the city. The definition of a liberal, as I see it, is two things. One: they are not tolerant of anything except their liberal views, and Two: They don't add up.

Grandpa always said that you could judge a person, or a statement, or a theory, or a belief, by whether or not it added up. For instance, being against the death penalty for our most despicable criminals, but being for abortion of precious, innocent, unborn babies, doesn't add up.

Brother-in-law is against hunting because he says he is against killing animals. But he eats meat. He uses leather belts and wallets. So he is paying others to kill animals for his use.

He catches and kills fish. He boils live crawfish and crabs to death. He uses roach poison on roaches, and ant poison on ants, and garden poison in the garden. It doesn't add up.

Brother-in-law is against private ownership of firearms. He says that he will vote for gun confiscation, because if it will save only one life, it will be worth it. The trouble is, that although guns are used in approximately one hundred and fifty thousand crimes a year, they are used by law-abiding citizens to prevent over two million crimes a year. Getting rid of guns wouldn't reduce murders and rapes; it would greatly increase them.

In a life or death conflict in which a two-hundred pound man attacks a one hundred and twenty pound woman, disarming the victim woman by preventing her from having a handgun, might save the life of the two hundred pound attacker. To a liberal, that is a life saved. To the victim, that is her life forfeited. It doesn't add up.

Rich liberals and high politicians live in protected communities and have armed bodyguards. They aren't fighting to have guns taken away from their bodyguards, just from the poor innocent citizens who can't afford protected communities or armed bodyguards.

The founders of our nation recognized that the citizens of a country cannot be free unless they can protect themselves and their property. Therefore, they recognized gun ownership by citizens as the cornerstone of freedom.

Brother-in-law would give up our freedom for what? It doesn't add up.

Brother-in-law would support a president who breaks the law, if that president will support the liberal agenda. It won't add up.

But I've got hope for my brother-in-law, because of one thing. He was smart enough to marry my sister. I won't be surprised if he learns a thing or two from her as time goes on.

He might even get to where things add up.

Chapter Fifty-Two
The Puppet

Grandpa used to work in his workshop quite a bit after work and on weekends. He built muzzle loaders, and made wood carvings, and repaired chairs, and things like that.

Down the road from Grandpa's was an old shack of a rent house that was usually rented to the kind of people who stayed there until their rent was due and then left without paying it.

For a while, the rent house was occupied by a mother, her son, and her daughter. The son was a wild, unfriendly boy, who stayed in trouble, but the daughter was a kind, gentle, good-natured little girl with a speech problem, who was a slow learner.

The little girl would walk to Grandpa's house and wait outside his workshop until Grandpa got home from work, and then would keep Grandpa company until he went into the house for supper.

The little girl chose not to talk to Grandma, I don't know why. But while she was with Grandpa, she never stopped talking. Mostly, she would make up fantasy stories about a princess and a prince, or a daddy who was coming to take care of her.

One day she asked Grandpa to make her a puppet, and of course, he did. It was just a little wooden puppet with articulated arms and legs, and strings to make it move.

Soon after Grandpa gave the puppet to the little girl, the little family moved out of the rent house and left no forwarding address.

Many years passed and Grandpa grew old and died. A visitation was held on the night before the funeral, and on the Sunday after the funeral, we had a memorial service for Grandpa at our little church.

At the memorial service, the church was packed with important people who got up one by one and told things about Grandpa, like how he had been a deacon in the church, and how he had served on the school board for many years, and things like that.

Towards the end of the service a kind, soft-spoken lady got up and went to the front to speak. No one knew who she was, but she was carrying a little wooden puppet.

The little lady said, "When I was young I had a hard time." She stuttered a little, but not too bad. "My mama was a tramp and was mean. My brother was hateful and very bad to me. I couldn't go to school because all of the kids teased me, and I was a slow learner, and couldn't pass out of the first grade. I didn't have a daddy, and I didn't have anybody who would even listen to me until we moved into a house down the road from Grandpa's. I would watch for Grandpa to get home and go in his workshop, and I would go to see him every day. I know now that I was probably a nuisance, but I didn't know it then, and Grandpa never let on that I was.

I could tell Grandpa all my worries, and all my dreams, and he never once thought that I was silly. One day I asked Grandpa to make me a puppet, and he did. It was the only thing that anybody ever made for me.

Then we moved. We went first one place and then another. My momma got real mean, and my brother hurt me worse and worse. The only thing I had to talk to was that puppet that Grandpa made for me.

I finally got big enough to get out on my own, and I got a job helping at the "Goodwill" store in a town. They found me a place to stay, and things began to get better. I learned to read and write, and do numbers.

Through it all, my little puppet was there. He listened to all my worries, and stories, and dreams, and he never once thought I was silly.

I saw in the newspaper that Grandpa had died, and that this memorial service would be held today. So I came to tell how great a man Grandpa was, and how lucky I was to have had him for a friend."

Then she cried a little and sat down. The pastor's wife went over and sat by her and held her in her arms.

The senator spoke next, but everybody was still crying with the little lady and didn't hear what he had to say.

When the gentle little lady retired, she move into our neighborhood, and regularly attended our church. I've been to her house. On her mantel sits a little wooden puppet with articulated arms and legs. His strings are long gone. His paint is mostly worn off. But he sits there with his legs dangling over the edge of the mantel, listening with rapt attention to every worry, dream, or silly story that the gentle little lady needs to tell.

Chapter Fifty-Three
The Heritage

My aunt was tight-lipped and had a deep frown on her face as she put the breakfast on the table. The discussion was over and she had lost. It's not that she was an anti-hunter, she wasn't. She was a non-hunter. She had tried hunting with my uncle several times, but just didn't like the hardships that a hunter is willing to go through to hunt. Her grandparents had hunted, but her parents had broken the heritage when they moved to the city before she was born. Now her baby, who came along much later than the others, was poised to go on the first hunt of the muzzle-loading season for deer.

My little cousin and my uncle ate quickly, hugged my aunt, picked up their flintlock rifles, left through the back door, crossed the yard and went into the woods. Not a word was spoken as they walked quietly through the woods. It would be daylight soon and they wanted to be in their stands and ready at first light.

As they approached the first stand, my uncle admitted to himself that he was tight-lipped and anxious about the child's first real hunt also. But she had earned the right. He grinned to himself as he thought how much she was like her mother, who was a handsome strong-willed woman, who knew right from wrong, and had her feet planted firmly in the church.

They had promised their daughter that she would have the same rules and privileges that the boys had and that when she could load and shoot the flintlock accurately and safely, and when she had passed the hunter safety course, she could go on a real hunt.

Trouble is, some promises are hard to keep. True enough, she could handle the beautiful flintlock rifle that Grandpa had made especially for her.

The rifle was several inches taller than she was. She couldn't shoot it off-hand yet, but she was accurate from a rest. Uncle asked her to load it light, but he could tell from the crack it made when she shot, that she was loading full loads. My uncle had to admit, that though thin, she was stronger than the boys were at that age, and more serious, too.

When my uncle and my cousin reached the first stand, she went up the tree like a cat and immediately lowered the light rope she had brought to pull the flintlock up with.

My uncle checked the flintlock. The pan was empty and a plug was in the vent hole. He tied the rope to the rifle and she pulled it up. He waved in the darkness but supposed she probably didn't see it as he set out walking for the next stand.

My uncle and my aunt had promised never to play favorites among the children, and they didn't. But he thought to himself, "A girl child is special. Somehow they get deep into your heart. You don't know how you became so thoroughly wrapped around their little finger, but it must have happened early on, because you've never known it to be otherwise."

My uncle fretted in his stand all morning, straining his ears to hear the woof-boom of the girl's flintlock, but no shot came.

Before noon, uncle climbed down and started back to my cousin's stand. He worried all the way back, "Now she'll not like hunting because she didn't see any deer. She'll be a non-hunter and the heritage will be broken."

My uncle reached my cousin's stand and waited while she lowered the flintlock through the limbs to the ground. He checked it and the pan had been emptied and the plug was in the vent. He knew she would do that before she lowered the rifle to the ground, but a rule never broken in our family was to check the safety condition of any gun that you pick up.

She came down the tree like a squirrel, and hugged his neck, and kissed him on the cheek.

His worries disappeared when she excitedly said, "I saw a fox and a squirrel. But that board up there is hard. Tomorrow I'm bringing a pillow."

Chapter Fifty-Four

Punkin

Punkin and Brother-in-law have been married for six glorious years. Oh, there were a few rough spots at first, because there were a few things Brother-in-law didn't know about then.

He thought she was going to do the cooking and the house cleaning. Then he thought she was going to do part of the cooking and house cleaning. Then he thought she would do part of either the cooking or the cleaning; but she cleared up that misconception.

She's a good provider. She's got two college degrees and a good paying job. And, she's in church every time the door is open. And sings in the choir.

She is a good hunter, too. I think it all started when Grandpa gave her a flintlock rifle that he made for her just before he died. She was five years old. It's a beautiful rifle, reliable, and very accurate.

I don't think she has set that flintlock down more than about twice since she has been married, it seems like.

Brother-in-law never knew her grandpa, but I take it he thinks Grandpa was ten feet tall and had a dog that was as big as a full-grown buffalo.

Brother-in-law made the mistake of saying that he would go anywhere Punkin wanted on their honeymoon, long as she paid for it. So they went grizzly bear hunting in Canada.

It was a nice trip. Just not much privacy with both of them and the guide in a two-man pup tent. And I understand that the guide had a strong aversion to bathing and had never heard of deodorant.

Brother-in-law thinks about that trip every time he cleans the den and has to clean around that monster grizzly rug with its huge mouth wide open. But the meat was good. Brother-in-law has got a bunch of good grizzly recipes.

I still tease her about having to shoot the grizzly twice. She says she didn't have to shoot twice, that it would have died before it reached them. And the only reason that she wasted the second arrow was because the guide had gone hysterical.

Yep, she's a good hunter. They haven't had to buy meat in six years. She even gave birth to their first set of twins at the deer camp. I asked her, "How was it?"

She said, "Nothing to it."

But I bet the other hunters thought there was something to it. She was late taking three of them out to their stands the next morning.

The twins are cute little girls, in their terrible twos now, and cutting their teeth on their first B B guns.

Punkin came in from work the other day and took off her stethoscope and coat and tie and slipped on a pair of camouflage coveralls. She said, "I might be a little late tonight. I'm going after that big buck in the swamp and it might slow me down dragging him out. Then I'll cape him out and get him mounted."

Brother-in-law said, "Where are we going to hang it? The wall space is all used up with your other heads."

Punkin said, "There's room for one more in the bedroom."

Brother-in-law said, "I can't hardly sleep in there now with all those eyes looking at me."

So she gave in to him like she always does. She said, "I'll have it mounted with its eyes shut." She is pretty intense about hunting, but he loves her and can't imagine living without her.

And she loves him, too. She told Brother-in-law that if he ever left her, she would kill him. And I know that she would do it with that flintlock rifle of hers.

One day I got up some courage and told her, "Punkin, there's more to life than hunting you know."

She said, "I know there is. I'm planning to take up bass fishing this summer."

Chapter Fifty-Five
The Race

Grandpa ran track at the state college where he got his degree in forestry.

Grandpa wasn't a speed burner. Speed burners ran in the sprints. Grandpa was what the coach called a "hoss". It took a "hoss" to run the four hundred and forty yard dash, also called the quarter mile. The modern equivalent in today's track meets is the four hundred meter race.

The coach said that you need the gift of speed to win the sprints (the 100 yard and 200 yard races) but for the 440-yard dash you need strength and determination and guts. Because toward the end of the 440 yard race, the oxygen in your body is used up faster than you can replace it by breathing, and pain and loss of muscle strength is the result. The layman's term for this phenomenon is that "the bear jumps on your back". And the harder you try, the bigger is the bear.

The distance races like the mile run and longer races are a different story and take different running strategies, but to make a long explanation short, you run below the bear-on-the-back speed.

Grandpa was selected to run the 440-yard dash because of his physical strength and mental toughness. The wise old track coach knew a "hoss" when he saw one.

Grandpa didn't always win his race. One certain thing about sports and about life in general is that there is always someone who is faster, or stronger, or smarter than you are, and they just might have as much guts and determination as you do.

But Grandpa always tried as hard as he could, and after a race if Grandpa had lost, the coach would put his hand on Grandpa's shoulder and say, "Hoss, you did your best." And Grandpa would know that he had done his best.

I always sat on the same pew with Grandpa in church, and lots of times I got to sit right next to him. And after Grandma died, I always sat next to him.

In track, the starter calls the runners in each race to the starting line and then says, "Take your mark, get set." Then, a blank pistol shot means "go". At "take your mark", each runner places his or her feet in the starting blocks and his or her hands as close to the starting line as possible without touching the line, by spreading the thumb and index finger of each hand out wide and up against the line.

Then, at "get set" the runner bunches their muscles for the start and focuses their entire attention on the starting gun. When the starting gun is fired, the runners spring out of the starting blocks with all their might and the race is on.

After Grandma died, I began to notice Grandpa in church when we were standing for a long prayer or song. He would put his hands on the back of the pew in front of his in a peculiar way, with the thumb and index finger spread wide apart like he was at the starting line of a race, and he would rock forward with his weight on his hands, and he would focus intently on something, I didn't know what.

At first I was worried that he was feeling weak and needed support to stand until I realized that he kept adjusting his fingers and thumbs until they were exactly perfect as close to the edge of the pew back as possible.

Grandpa was preparing to run a race and he was going to finish it with determination and guts, and when the bear jumped on his back, Grandpa was going to keep on to the finish line.

And when Grandpa crossed the finish line, Grandma was going to be cheering from the crowd, and the Big Coach was going to put his hand on Grandpa's shoulder and say, "Good race, old hoss. You did your best, my good and faithful servant."

Author's note:

After I wrote this chapter, I realized that the seed for this story probably had been planted in my subconscious mind by a moving tribute to the late Judge Leon Whitten, written by Tom Ayres, and published in our local newspaper. In the tribute, Tom Ayres used a track analogy, and was truly magnificent.

Chapter Fifty-Six
The Knife Collection

Grandpa collected pocketknives. He claimed he only collected "Case" brand knives, although he had a few "off-brands", he called them, in his collection. He must have had two hundred pocketknives in his big glass-topped display case.

Grandpa and my Dad would go to gun-and-knife shows together every once in a while. Dad said that Grandpa would find the most worn out pocketknife, or one with a broken blade, and he would buy it.

Dad said that he always told Grandpa, "That knife doesn't have any collector's value. It's worn out," or "It's missing a blade, or handle."

See, in knife collecting, the most valuable knives are usually the ones that haven't been used. Even sharpening them can lower the price. There are some exceptions for very rare knives, but most of the time within collectable knives, condition is a very important factor.

Grandpa would send an old broken knife that he had bought off to get fixed at the factory or to a knife repair place. My Dad would always say, "You could have bought a brand new knife for the money you have in that one."

But Grandpa knew what he liked and respected in a knife. He would look at one of his worn out knives and say, "That's honest wear on that knife. It hasn't been abused."

Oh, he had some beautiful knives in his collection. Like a pearl handled "Case" trapper, and an abalone shell handled "Case" three blade whittler, and a stag handled "Case" five blade sowbelly. Grandma had given most of the beautiful knives to him on birthdays and such. She always preferred shiny knives. And cost didn't matter to Grandma when she was buying a present for Grandpa. And Grandpa treasured the knives from Grandma.

Sometimes when Grandpa was going through his knife collection and rearranging them or whatever he did to them, my little sister would ask him a question like; which knife was his favorite?

He always chose the same one. It was an "off-brand" from the Sears and Roebuck catalog. My Grandpa's father had carried it all his life. It had one scale, handle I call it, replaced with metal. He said that my great, great, grandpa had put on that homemade handle for my great grandpa a long time ago. The remaining bone handle was worn smooth, but the blades were razor sharp. Grandpa would hold that knife, and maybe open a blade, and he would just sit quiet for a while.

Then my sister would ask him which was his second favorite and he would pick either the little "Case" three-bladed, bone handled knife, that the pastor who married him and Grandma gave to him, or the bone handled "Case" stockman that was the first knife that he ever bought. He said that he was about twelve years old when he bought the knife new for $4.95, which was just a nickel short of eight weeks allowance.

Grandpa said that he carried the stockman for over thirty years until one winter when the temperature in north Louisiana went down to five degrees and stayed below freezing for five days. When things finally thawed, all the pipes under the house were broken. Grandpa said that he crawled around on his belly in the narrow crawlspace under the house until he got the pipes fixed.

He said that when he crawled out from under the house and stood up he patted his left front pocket like he always did to make sure his knife was safe, but it was gone for the first time ever.

So Grandpa got a flashlight and went back under the house and looked and looked, but he couldn't find his knife. So then he borrowed a strong magnet, and tied it to a long cane pole and swept it through the sand under the house, and then pulled it back out. On the first try, he pulled out a ring that you clamp into a bull's nose to lead it around. On the second try, he pulled out his "Case" knife and he hasn't carried it since.

After that he carried an "off-brand" so that if he lost it he wouldn't be so worried. He still used the "Case" stockman to do the grafting and budding in his orchard. He used the third blade, which was always razor sharp, but so were the other two blades.

Then my sister would ask him, which is his next favorite? And he always picked a little stag handled three-blade knife made by J. A. Henckels in Germany. Grandpa said that little knife is real old, but that he didn't have a better knife in his whole collection.

He said that the little knife was given to him by his good friend, Jim, who he worked with for years. He said Jim bought the knife at a flea market. It had a missing master blade, so Grandpa sent it back to the Henckels factory in Germany, and in a couple of weeks it came back with a brand new master blade and a letter that said "No Charge."

My sister told Grandpa that the perfect little Henckels knife was her favorite.

When Grandpa died he gave the knife collection to my Dad, except that little Henckels. He gave that to my sister.

And you know Pentecostal women don't cut their hair, or wear jewelry, or makeup, and they don't wear trousers or men's clothes. Just dresses, or skirts and blouses, and most dresses and skirts don't have pockets on them, but my sister's do. If they don't when she buys them, she sews one on. And in the pocket she carries that perfect little Henckels pocketknife that Grandpa gave her. And every once in a while, she pats that pocket to make sure that little pocketknife is safe in there.

Epilogue

My Great-grandfather is a legend in our family. I never met him. He died long before I was born, well over fifty years ago.

Great-grandfather died when my mom was six years old, but she has vivid memories of him. At least, she used to have. Her mind is about gone now. But when she does remember something, it's usually something about Great-grandpa.

Great-grandfather was the founding father of our family, so to speak. His faith in God, his love of family, his love of nature, and his creative ability set an example that we all try to live up to.

Mom and a few other family members, who actually knew Great-grandfather, tried to write down some of the stories that they knew about him, and my uncle put them together in this book. But time passes so quickly and memories fade. I sometimes wonder if the stories are all true.

I know he was a good woodcarver because Mom and some of the others have beautiful things that he carved.

I know that he was a good hunter because I've seen the old picture albums that document some of his hunting trips.

I know that he was a good gun builder because I've seen the beautiful flintlock rifle that he made for my mom long ago.

Great-grandfather's fruit tree orchard still exists, and I've eaten fruit and pecans off of the old trees that he grafted a long time ago.

But what is legend, and what is fact? When you listen to stories about Great-grandfather, you get the impression that he was bigger than life. But pictures of him in the old albums are pictures of a rather plain-looking, average-sized man.

One story, often repeated, is that he lifted a huge brass bearing at the blacksmith shop that was never lifted before or since by any one man alone. And that he could lift a 120-pound weight over his head with either hand. But pictures of him are not of a physically big man.

So legends and reality sometimes get mixed up.

But Great-grandfather's faith in God and his moral strength is not in question. The proof of that is in our big family, all descendants of Great-grandfather. All of us know right from wrong, and we all are firmly in the church, and we all pray every day.

And we all go hunting every chance we get.

Printed in the United States
43458LVS00002B/220-318

9 781413 712551